EVERYTHING WE NEVER WANTED

Sienna Waters

Sienna Waters
© 2020 All Rights Reserved

All rights reserved. No part of this publication may be reproduced, distributed, or or transmitted in any form or by any means, without prior permission by the author except in the case of brief quotations for the purposes of review and non-commercial cases as per law.

This is a work of fiction. All characters and events exist solely in the author's imagination, and any resemblance to actual people, alive or dead, is pure coincidence. All characters are eighteen years of age or older.

Stay up to date with the latest news from Sienna Waters by following me on Twitter @WatersSienna!

To N.–
And the perfect balance
xxx

CHAPTER ONE

Alex rummaged through a box and pulled out a pink, wispy piece of material. "What about this?"

Libby shook her head and made a moue of disgust, so Alex went back to the box. She really didn't need this. She could feel the crusty spikes of sleep still in her eyes and her hands were shaking for want of some serious caffeine. Maybe she should put her foot down, but the ground was shaky enough that she didn't know if it was safe. Better to postpone the morning coffee than to risk another meltdown.

"This one!" Libby shrieked. She held up a yellow, frilly dress that Alex was fairly certain was supposed to be for parties or weddings or something.

"You sure?" she asked, doubtfully.

"Yip."

And Libby was so happy, beaming and bouncing around her new bedroom, that Alex almost let it go. There was a lot to be said for taking the easy road. Especially at seven in the morning when she'd just about kill to get back under her comforter. But… But she had responsibilities.

Even the word weighed on her, made her feel black and heavy and bleh.

"Man, you really think that's for school?"

Libby shrugged. "It's a special day dress. And the first day of second grade's a special day. Isn't it?"

The first day in second grade, first day in a new school, first day in public school for that matter. Alex scratched her nose. "Um, yeah," she agreed. "But then, what will the other kids be wearing? I mean, what if you wear a yellow dress and everyone else is in jeans or shorts?"

Libby pouted and Alex could feel a meltdown shimmering in the air. "I like this one," she said.

Christ, she needed coffee. She pushed back her short, dark hair, long enough now that it dangled in her eyes when she bent over the packing boxes. "Okay," she said. "I mean, I guess. If it's what you want."

"It is," Libby said.

Her little white teeth were like pearls, her arms were tanned from the summer sun and plump with childish dimples, and her smile was bright enough to light up the whole house. Alex couldn't help herself. She pulled the kid into a hug, squashing her tight until Libby wriggled and protested. Sometimes it hurt so bad to love her so much.

"Alright, alright," Alex said, freeing her finally. "I'm going to get breakfast started or you'll starve on your first day of school. Put that dress on and come down when you're done, 'kay?"

"Yes."

"Straight down when you're done. No time for playing or reading or anything else."

"Okay."

She'd learned pretty fast that when giving a seven year old instructions it was best to seal every possible loophole and foresee every contingency. Libby was pulling the dress over her dark curls as Alex left her to it.

In the kitchen, she contemplated eggs but seriously couldn't stomach the smell of cooking that early in the morning. She flipped the switch on the coffee machine and pulled out bowls and a battered cereal box instead. At least there was fresh milk.

The morning sun was bright and yellow, it was going to be another beautiful day. The back lawn was crisp and brown in patches after a summer of similar beautiful days. Her back lawn. Her house. Responsibilities again. She shuddered. The idea of it, of owning something so permanent made her feel queasy. But it had been the right thing to do.

The right thing to do.

Her stupid life at the moment was full of right things and wrong things and somehow they never seemed to match up to things she wanted and things she didn't. Things had been so much easier before.

She pulled her mobile out of the pocket of her shorts, scrolling through her messages as the coffee machine bleeped and buzzed and hissed and eventually began to flow.

Wish you were here?

The text wasn't signed, but it didn't have to be. The accompanying picture showed a small cove, ocean turquoise and mirror-still, sand so white it was dazzling, and a palm bent over far enough that the woman in the picture could use it as a bench.

Wish you were here? The question mark made it a question, though it could just as easily be a statement.

Alex couldn't think of anywhere she'd rather be. A whirling started in her stomach, her eyes stung with tears of unfairness. The coffee machine beeped again and little feet pounded on the stairs. For a moment there she'd almost heard the ocean, the hushing of waves, almost smelled the salt tang of it. Stupid Evie. Even though it wasn't really her fault. Even though the understanding had been there, unspoken, but still there, that Alex would be back. That she'd return. After it was all over.

"Yay! Cereal!"

Blinking back the tears, Alex sniffed. "Seriously kid? It's just cereal."

"Yeah, but Anna never let me have cereal. She said that I had to have good nutritiousness before school."

"Good nutrition," Alex corrected unconsciously. "Did she? And I suppose she'd have let you wear a yellow princess dress to school too, huh?"

Libby laughed like tinkling bells. "My old school had a uniform, silly. And Anna hanged it on my bedroom door every night at bedtime."

"Hung it," corrected Alex again. "I bet she did."

She grabbed the cool container of milk out of the fridge. Anna, Libby's nanny, had been perfect, as far as Alex could tell. She'd also been far from pleased at being fired. But then, paying someone a monthly salary that was more than what Alex generally made in a year to look after a kid that was in school for eight hours a day seemed a little much. As had paying school fees that could have funded the debt of a small nation.

So things had changed.

She'd done the right thing.

Sometimes she needed to repeat that to herself like a mantra that kept her breathing.

"Alex... A-lex..."

She shook herself out of it and turned to pour milk onto Libby's cereal. "Eat up, kiddo. The school bus will be here soon."

"I can't believe I get to go to school on a bus," Libby said, grasping her spoon. "And by myself. This place is the greatest."

The school bus had been the talking point of the weekend and Alex had no clue why the girl was so obsessed with being able to take it. But since it had seemed to take the sting out of starting at a whole new school where Libby knew nobody, she hadn't really questioned it. And she guessed that independence had been in short supply when Libby had been chauffeured around by a nanny.

"It's yellow, you know. The bus, I mean. Like your dress."

Libby rolled her eyes. "Like I wouldn't know that. Everyone knows that school buses are yellow. And even they're magic sometimes."

"Magic?" Alex frowned. She poured her much-needed coffee. It seemed like Libby might be in for an unpleasant surprise in the bus department.

"Yeah, like on TV, there's this show called The Magic School

Bus and..."

Alex tuned out as she sipped her coffee. If she closed her eyes she could almost imagine she was on the beach with Evie. Almost.

The development smelled like fresh cut grass and somewhere a sprinkler jetted and splattered. So suburban that it could have been a painting. But the right thing, the right choice, Alex reminded herself yet again.

"It's here! It's here!"

A yellow bus chugged around the corner and Alex barely held on to Libby's hand. "You gonna be okay, kid?" she asked, suddenly wondering if maybe she should have driven her.

"Yes, yes, let me go, Alex."

She was shaking her hand to break free as the bus pulled to a halt. Alex stooped down, clasping the hot, wriggling body to her one more time. "Just tell the teacher to call me if you need me," she said. "For anything. Anytime you like. Promise?"

"Promise," Libby said, finally pulling out of Alex's arms. "Bye!" And she was bounding off to the bus.

Alex sighed as she watched her go. It was a weird feeling. Relief at finally having her sense of responsibility lifted for a few hours. And... Well, loneliness, she supposed. She'd gotten used to having Libby and her chattering around. Fear too maybe. She hoped that Libby would be okay, that strangers would take care of her, that children would like her. There was a fierce desire to protect the child that she hadn't really counted on.

"Cute kid."

She turned around and saw a half-naked man jogging up the driveway of the house next door. He wiped sweat from his brow, stopped, and grinned at her.

"I'm Doug, and you're the new neighbor," he said. "And your kid, she's super cute."

Alex almost said thank you. But then she didn't. She'd done enough of the right thing in the last few weeks, months even. So she didn't thank Doug.

Instead, she said: "Oh, she's not mine."

And watched as Doug's face fell into a picture of worried concern.

CHAPTER TWO

"This was a terrible idea."

Fran just laughed and picked up the pace. Kat gritted her teeth and pushed herself a little harder, managing to match the other woman but only barely.

The trail was soft underfoot, each footstep launching a cloud of dust as they ran. The early morning sun dappled through the trees and it was almost beautiful. Right up until Kat took into account the fact that her legs were on fire and her lungs might well be about to explode.

"Here."

Fran stopped at a crossroads in the trail, passing over a water-bottle that Kat took gratefully. She glugged a few mouthfuls before she caught her breath enough to say again: "This was a terrible idea."

"This was a fantastic idea," Fran said, her face wrinkling into a smile as she took the water back and had a mouthful herself. She started walking, slower now, her blonde ponytail bobbing.

"In what kind of sick world was this a fantastic idea?" Kat asked, able to talk now they were walking.

"In the kind of world where this is the first day of school."

"Which is why I should still be sleeping before getting up to have a decent breakfast and a calm and leisurely drive to work."

"Psh." Fran tossed the water-bottle from one hand to another. "First of all, you've been in school all week preparing for those kids, so if it's not done now it's not going to get done. Second of all, you're going to start the year feeling high and full of energy and good thoughts after your morning run. And third of all, don't tell me that you slept last night."

Kat shrugged.

"I could hear you tossing and turning through the wall," said Fran. "Worried about your first day back, huh?"

"I just—I haven't slept well since… well, since."

"Since bitch number one left you for bitch number two?" Fran asked.

"Fran!" But Kat was grinning. Sometimes it was nice to have someone as completely on her side as Fran was. Someone who put a roof over her head when she had nowhere to stay. Someone who let her cry. Someone who pushed her to go running on the first day of school.

"Sorry, babe. But it's true."

"It's not. Jen's not a bitch. She's my wife."

"Ex-wife."

"Whatever." Signing the divorce papers hadn't been the greatest moment of her life. "It's… a combination of everything, I suppose."

A year ago today she'd had everything. A job she loved, a house she adored, a wife she doted on. The only thing missing had been a child of her very own. But they'd been working on it. Discussing it. Yet here she was, wandering through the woods, lost and broke and sleeping in her best friend's spare room. From perfect to shattered in the space of three hundred and sixty five days.

Fran clutched her arm. "You're going to be fine, Kat. You know you are. It's getting a little bit better every day, isn't it?"

"Sure," Kat said, but she didn't know who needed to hear that more, herself or Fran.

"And don't tell me that your life isn't going to get insanely better the second that you see all those shining little faces lining up and waiting for the greatest second grade teacher in the world."

"Greatest?" Kat said as they rounded the trail and Fran's car came into view, sparkling and shiny clean and new.

"Greatest," Fran said, giving Kat's arm another squeeze. "You're amazing at your job and you know you are. There's no point denying every good thing about yourself." She pulled her car key out of her arm-band pocket. "I know the divorce was hard on you, Kat. But this is a big day."

"It is?" It didn't feel like a big day. It felt like a sad day. A heartbreaking day. Yet another milestone passing by that could have, should have, been shared with her loving wife.

"It is," Fran said defiantly. "This is a new start. A clean start. Today is the first day of the rest of your life."

Even Kat laughed at that. Americans were always so robustly optimistic about everything, and it was a character trait that she loved. She'd lived in the country since she was fifteen, brought from Germany by her parents, and she'd never, ever regretted the move.

"I mean it, Kat. First day of the rest of your life. Get used to it. Things will change from today, mark my words."

"Fine, fine," Kat said, still smiling.

The car beeped as Fran unlocked the doors and Kat climbed in. The first day of the rest of her life. A nice idea. But unlikely to be true. Fran was adjusting the rear-view mirror, her profile regular, the morning sun catching the down on her cheeks. They'd been friends for years now, Fran was the sister she'd never had. But she hadn't had the heart to tell her.

To tell her that this could be the very last first day of school. That the financial situation was wobbly enough that it was starting to topple. That Kat just couldn't afford to do the job she loved for much longer.

Fran would be almost as destroyed by the idea as Kat was. That was how close they were.

"Sing along," Fran ordered as she turned up the radio.

An old Abba song blared out. The first day of the rest of her life. She wished it to be true. As she started to sing with Fran, she let herself believe it. Just for a little while.

The car drew into the parking space with a groan and a clank and seemed to sigh with relief when Kat switched off the engine. For a second she thought about the soft humming of Fran's new car and was jealous. A car that ran and didn't slurp down oil and gas like they were smoothies would be nice.

But well out of her price range.

As was a new outfit for the first day of school.

She got out of the car, smoothing down her pencil skirt and straightening her blouse. She'd tried to jazz the outfit up with some red beads but she wasn't entirely sure that the effort had been worth it. She pulled her bag out of the passenger seat and slammed the door.

Deep breath. First day. She could do this. She had had butterflies in her stomach on the first day of school for, Jesus, twenty eight years now, from the first day of kindergarten, through elementary and high school, college, teacher training, and now teaching. Everything had always turned out just fine, and there was no reason that it wouldn't today.

Today is not a special day, she told herself as she walked through the parking lot. Today is just another day. It's not the first day of the rest of your life, it's not your last first day of school, it's just a day. The butterflies fluttered a little harder.

Her classroom was pristine, the walls already covered with posters and bright pictures. Her name was written in big letters on the whiteboard, Ms. Stein. She just hoped that all the new kids she was getting would be able to read it.

A peek out of the window showed children already playing in the playground, shrieking and laughing as they saw friends. Some of the quieter ones stood back by the fence. New kids, she guessed. But they'd be incorporated soon enough. At this age kids didn't remain loners for long.

As she watched, another school bus came and disgorged its load at the front gates. One by one the kids hopped off, tanned faces shining like berries. Her heart filled up just seeing them, her new charges, children that she'd help to shape and grow. People she could have a lasting impact on.

A little girl was the last one off the bus, waving a cheerful goodbye to the driver as she jumped down the last step. Kat sighed. Honestly, some parents were beyond her. Who the hell sent a kid to school on her first day in a bright yellow princess dress?

"Ready for the hordes?"

She turned around to see Trisha Benson, the third grade teacher that occupied the class next to hers, popping her head around the door.

"Ready as I'll ever be," she grinned.

Trisha glanced down at her watch. "Then you'd better start your countdown. You're on your last minute of freedom. Last chance to change your mind."

Kat laughed. "I can't run away now, where would I go?"

"Tahiti," Trisha said immediately. She was still laughing as she walked away.

Tahiti. As if. Like she'd ever do anything even vaguely as exciting and exotic as that. Plain Kat, boring Kat, dependable Kat.

The bell rang, a startling tinny noise. Kat took a deep breath and moved to the door. Time to welcome in her brand new second grade class. Time for a brand new start. Her butterflies fluttered one last time and disappeared into the ether as a herd of footsteps clattered along the hallway.

CHAPTER THREE

Doug's house was minimalistic, white and grey and somehow very, very calming. Alex followed him down the hall to the kitchen, her nose twitching at the smell of coffee.

"So, tell me the deets," Doug said, pulling out two mugs. "That kid isn't yours. And... What? You stole a baby? Did you steal a baby?"

Alex laughed. "No. No, I didn't."

"Swear to God."

"Swear to God."

"Shame," Doug said, passing her a cup of coffee. "I was already picturing myself in the Lifetime movie of the week."

"Libby is my niece." She felt the heaviness again, the responsibility, along with the awkward anticipation of what was always an uncomfortable situation. No matter how many times she had to explain it never got easier. And she knew that Doug would end up feeling bad. People who asked always did.

"Your niece," he said, raising an eyebrow and clinking his coffee cup against hers. "That sounds like a complicated situation that's potentially going to lead to an awkward conversation that you might not want to have."

"Got it in one." He grinned at her, dimple in one cheek, his shaved head still slightly beaded with sweat. It was nice to be understood, nice to not feel guilty about the story she carried inside.

"In that case, feel free not to tell your nosey neighbor about it," he said. "What brings you to the neighborhood then?"

"Ach, it's all connected," Alex said. And suddenly she didn't mind telling him, wanted to tell him even. There was something about him, a calm quietness that made her want to open up.

"Again, you don't have to talk to me." He was leaning against the sink, casually sipping at his coffee.

"My sister, Libby's mother, died in a car accident about six months ago."

"I'm so sorry."

"We weren't particularly close," Alex said. It hurt, sure it did. But she'd only seen Claire once every couple of years at best, so it was easy most days to pretend that she wasn't gone at all. Except for Libby's constant presence.

"Still."

"Still," she agreed. "And that's the hard part. Everything else you can probably guess. I'm Libby's guardian now, this is a nice suburb, good schools, sprinklers, nice neighbors, blah, blah, blah."

"What about Libby's dad?" Doug asked, curious.

Alex shrugged. "No idea who he is or where he is or anything else. Claire was... independent. Like me, I guess, but in different ways. She was a lawyer, successful too. She wanted a kid, so she had one. I'm not sure I ever even really questioned who the father was."

"Really not close then."

"Not close," Alex said. And she wondered if they could have been. But even as kids she and Claire had argued so often that at times their bedroom had been a war-zone. "So here I am. Living in suburbia with a child and a house and a car and, well, that's it. I haven't had time to buy the dog yet."

Doug laughed. "I get it. Suburbia isn't for everyone. But why come here if it's not what you like?"

"Because it was the right thing to do," Alex said. "Because

Libby was so torn up after Claire died, because I wanted her to have some stability, because despite it all, I really do love her."

"Despite it all?"

Alex shook her head and drank some coffee to give herself a moment to think. "This isn't me," she said finally. "It's not my life."

"What is your life?"

She grinned now, remembering Evie, the beach, the palm tree. "Traveling," she said. "I've traveled since I was twenty one. Never had a home, moved on when I felt like it, worked behind a bar or in a hostel when I needed cash, lived on the beach. That's my life."

"A life that you had to give up when your sister died."

"What other choice did I have?"

But that was a lie. She'd had a choice. She just hadn't been able to decide any other way. She'd looked at Libby and hadn't been able to turn her away, hadn't wanted to. She'd put herself in this situation. She'd been the fun aunt, appearing with arms full of presents, letting Libby have ice cream for breakfast. The learning curve that was slowly turning her into a parent was a steep one.

"Do you regret it?" Doug asked.

Alex narrowed her eyes and put her coffee cup down, folding her arms. "Are you a cop?" she asked.

"Nope."

"Then why do I feel suddenly like I'm being interrogated."

Doug grinned and it was disarming and she wasn't really mad. "I'm a psychologist," he said. "And I'm sorry, I get a little carried away. I didn't mean to 'therapize' you. Comes with the territory, I'm afraid."

She picked up her coffee again. "No, it's fine. I could probably use a little therapy."

"It certainly sounds like you've been through a lot of changes. And maybe that they weren't all good ones, at least for you."

"I just... I feel so responsible now. So boring. So grown up. I feel like I had to give my life up. But at the same time, I see

Libby's face every morning and I know that it's worth it. I... I get confused."

Doug laughed. "We all do, my dear. You're not alone in that. Want another cup?"

Alex looked down to see that her cup was close to empty. "Sure. It's not like I've got anything better to do."

"That's flattering," Doug said, taking her cup. "Don't have a job then?"

"Nope. Claire left enough money that we probably couldn't spend it all if we tried. So I don't really need to." She looked down at the floor and felt her face flush. "Actually, I kind of need to work on that. I know I should be doing something, I just... I don't know what the hell that is. Can you see me being a housewife?"

"Honestly? Not really."

"Then I need to come up with a career plan. One that lets me look after Libby as well as she deserves. And one that keeps me busy."

Doug gave her the cup back and raised his own. "To new starts then," he said.

"To new starts," Alex agreed. She sipped the coffee and closed her eyes. "I could marry you for coffee this good every morning."

"You'd be barking up the wrong tree, dear," Doug said. "I'm as gay as they come."

"Ah, um, me too." She blushed again thinking of Evie. Not that they were together. Just that sometimes they... When it was convenient they were. And now Evie wanted her to come back and she didn't know how to make her believe that it wasn't an option anymore. As much as she'd tried to explain, Evie just wasn't buying it. Not that she saw herself with Evie forever. Not that she saw herself with anyone forever.

"I feel guilty," she said, out of nowhere. It felt good to say it.

"Guilty?"

"For everything. For wanting Libby to be happy, for loving her. But for wanting my old life back as well."

"It can take a long time after a major life change to make things make sense again," Doug said. "It's not an unusual feeling." He hesitated, then said: "I can recommend a colleague if you'd like? Someone you could talk to?"

His dimples were very cute, Alex thought. And his patients must find him so easy to open up to. She shook her head. "Not just now. I want to work out some things by myself first."

"Offer's always open," Doug said. "As is the offer of babysitting. If you ever need a hand, just say the word. I work from home so I'm around most of the time. I love kids and I know how valuable it can be to have a little time off every now and again. So if it helps, I'm here, just knock."

"I'll have to run it by Libby first."

"I'll be prepared to audition, don't worry," Doug said.

Alex smiled. For the first time since moving she thought that maybe she might be able to do this. Libby was already seven. It wouldn't be that long until she was off to college and Alex could do whatever she liked. And maybe they could travel anyway, in the vacations at least. Libby might want to go to high school abroad. There were options.

Her life wasn't over. It was just different now. She tried to remember that. But as soon as she saw a picture like the one Evie had sent, she forgot all over again.

"You're not a bad person," Doug said. She looked at him and he grinned. "A lot of people need to hear that. You've been forced to put your own interests and life aside to help someone else. Having the occasional regret doesn't make you a bad person. It makes you normal."

Alex smiled and thanked him. She just wished that she could believe him.

"And you never know," he said with a wink. "Sometimes a new start can bring all kinds of surprises. Things do have a tendency to work out for the best in the long run."

And that she truly didn't believe.

CHAPTER FOUR

The bell rang and there was the familiar sound of little feet shuffling and butts wiggling on chairs. Kat held up both her hands until her class was completely silent. She almost smiled as she saw the strain in their faces, desperately trying to keep still and not flee the classroom. The temptation of the school bell was great, Kat knew that. But discipline was important.

"Alright, class. We've been over the rules for the lunchroom and the playground. But just as a reminder."

She pointed a finger at the whiteboard.

"We will be respectful to our schoolmates," chorused the children.

She moved her finger down a row.

"We will solve problems with words, not with fights."

Down to the next.

"We will include everyone who wants to play."

"Very good. Now line up by the door, please."

She could already hear kids from the other classes pounding down the corridors. Not something she approved of. Her children were quietly getting into line and she grinned. They'd already got the measure of her, they already knew she wasn't to be messed with. It was amazing how quickly and how well kids could judge adults.

"Okay, and I think we'll have..." She looked up and down the line and chose the boy who looked most responsible. "Robbie. Robbie, will you lead the class to lunch, please?"

He gave a gap-toothed grin and went to the head of the line. Kat took a breath, then opened the door. It was all very well controlling the kids inside her classroom, but outside of it they were more of an unknown quantity. Robbie set off at a march and like a snake unwinding the others followed him. Okay, so he was speed-walking, practically waddling as he hurried down the corridor, but there was some sense of order.

Kat laughed and picked up her own lunch-box from her desk before repairing to the teacher's lounge.

"And to think," Trisha said as Kat pulled up a seat at her table. "You could have been in Tahiti by now."

"I'm pretty sure it takes more than three hours to fly to the Pacific islands," Kat said. "Besides, who would have taken roll call and handled the playground rules?"

Trisha laughed. "True that." She opened up a tupperware containing what looked like the remains of Chinese take-out.

Kat's stomach rumbled and she opened up her own box. Bologna sandwiches on plain white bread. Cheap. Tomorrow would be PB and J. Equally cheap. Not exactly gourmet food. She had to swallow down her disappointment before taking a bite and chewing slowly to make it last.

"So, how was your summer?" she asked politely.

"Well, Kev and I took the kids to Disney, which was the shitshow that you'd imagine," Trisha said. "Honestly, I could use a vacation after my vacation. Going from the kids here to the kids at home ain't no kind of break. You?"

Kat shrugged. It was alright for Trisha. Her husband was a software analyst at a big company. They had money for two cars and clothes and Disney trips. Not that Trisha was any less devoted to her students than Kat. But... having two incomes definitely helped keep things together.

"Nothing special," she said.

Trisha raised an eyebrow. "No new beau on the horizon?"

At this Kat had to laugh. "No, Trish. Not even close. Besides,

I've only been divorced for four months."

"You know what they say. You fall off the horse, you get straight back on that sucker."

"Good advice for horses," Kat said. "Less so for spouses."

The lounge was filling up now. Trisha moved her chair a little closer. "So what did you do then, honey? Don't tell me you spent all summer moping around?"

Kat rubbed her eyes. There was no make-up to be disturbed. Not today. She was in half a mind to deflect the question but told herself that she didn't need to be ashamed. Shouldn't be ashamed.

"I, uh, spent the summer working," she said. She left a beat, then added: "Fast food for the win, eh?"

Trisha sent her a sympathetic smile. "Don't think you're the only one, honey. It's a sad state of affairs."

"What do you mean?" The bologna sandwich tasted an awful lot like cardboard.

"Look around you," said Trisha. "You see Anne White?"

Kat craned her neck to look around then shook her head.

"You wouldn't," Trisha said. "She quit over the summer to go work for some computer company. What about Joe? See him anywhere?"

Kat didn't even bother to look around this time. "Where did he defect to?"

"Corporate job doing accountancy I heard," said Trisha.

"That's a shame. The kids loved him. And there aren't enough decent math teachers, or frankly, enough male elementary school teachers."

"Tell me about it," Trisha said. "And Annie White was a qualified music teacher too, so that's another loss. But likely they didn't exactly have much choice in the matter. Budget cuts, minimum wage salaries, working weekends and vacations and paying for classroom supplies out of pocket, this is no job for someone young and just out of school with a ton of college debt."

Kat sighed and Trisha looked at her.

"And maybe no job for a recent divorcee who has to go it alone either," she added. "But we'd hate to lose you, Kat. I'd hate to lose you."

"I'm a harridan," Kat said with a grin. "I make trouble in staff meetings, any kid that's not in my class is terrified of me, and I've got the loudest voice this side of the Mississippi."

"You're old school," Trisha said. "Like me. Know how to keep discipline. There's nothing wrong with that. We need more teachers like you. If we can keep you on board that is."

Kat pushed her lunch-box away. "I don't know," she said honestly. "I just don't. When we were a two income family this was fine, but…"

"But you need to think about yourself and the future," said Trisha. "And as much as you love teaching, and I see that you do, it just doesn't get the bills paid." She took a forkful of noodles. "What would you do instead?"

What could she do? Another shrug. "Not a damn clue. This is really all I know how to do. Teach."

"Corporate training," Trisha said. "Plenty of money in that. And you speak German, so you could always do private tutoring."

"Tutoring."

Trisha rolled her eyes. "My daughter has a math tutor. Guy's still in college. And given what I pay him and the amount of students he could potentially have in his free time I'm pretty sure he's making twice what I am. Tutors demand high rates if they get good results."

The thought of not being in her classroom, of not being surrounded by kids, felt strange. Lonely even. "I don't know. I'll think about it. I guess I'm not going anywhere until the end of semester. Maybe even the end of the school year. I've got a little time to think about it."

Trisha reached across and squeezed her hand. "I hope you can stay. But I understand if you can't. You're not the only one in that boat. In the meantime, if there's something I can do, you just say the word. Us old-timers have to stick together."

"Keep your fingers crossed for a miracle then," Kat said. "Coffee?"

"I'd die without it."

Kat grinned and pushed her chair back to get in line for the coffee machine. At least that was free. No one had yet been dumb enough to try and take free caffeine out of the teacher's lounge.

She was just putting two hot cups on the table and pushing one toward Trisha when there was a knock at the door. A knock generally meant a student and since she was close and already on her feet, she was the one that opened the door.

"Ms. Stein," said a small girl.

Kat smiled at her. She knew the kid, had been her teacher two years ago. "What is it, Alison?"

"The lunch monitor sent me to get you," the girl said, hopping from one leg to the other. "Your class was fighting and then someone cried and then..." She gasped in a deep breath. "And then the lunch monitor said that they were in trouble and that I should get you." A brief hesitation, then a nod as the child remembered more. "Oh, and you should go to your classroom."

Kat thanked the child and went to grab her coffee. "Duty calls," she said to Trisha.

As she walked down the corridor she wondered which of her kids had been fighting. She'd put money on it being Jayden, a curly haired boy that looked like butter wouldn't melt in his mouth. The innocent looking ones always ended up being the most trouble.

And when she opened her classroom door she was indeed greeted by Jayden's wide blue eyes and doleful expression. And by someone else. Standing next to him, frilly yellow princess dress ripped and dirty, was Olivia Blakely.

CHAPTER FIVE

Alex gripped the steering wheel and gritted her teeth waiting for the light to change. As soon as there was the first flicker of green she was off, tires squealing as she peeled away. Only when she got to the school gates did she finally slow down. Pulling into the parking lot she took a last second to take a deep breath. Whatever it was, it couldn't be that bad, right?

She was cursing herself as she walked to the school building. Who was she to know what the right thing was? She never should have pulled Libby out from her old school. She never should have moved her. She never should have let her take the bus alone.

It was moments like this, moments when her whole body seemed to be on the verge of turning inside out with anxiety, that she knew that she loved Libby more than she'd ever loved anyone ever before. It was strange, to have love confirmed by fear like that. But she swore to God, if anyone or anything had hurt her baby she'd tear off someone's head.

"Ma'am? Ma'am? Can I help you?"

A security guard was running down the pavement. Alex barely paused.

"Ma'am? I'm going to have to ask you to stop."

If anything, she went faster, peering through windows, looking for a dark-haired little girl in a yellow dress. Whatever the hell the school had called her for, Libby had better be okay. Better than okay.

"Ma'am!"

The tone of the guard's voice paused her. Paused her for long enough that she realized it would probably be more efficient to ask for directions.

"I need Ms. Stein's office."

"And you are?"

The security guard had caught up now, a robust woman with sweat stains under her pits and a dragon tattoo on her forearm. The kind of woman that in another time, another place, Alex might just have made a run for. Rough and ready, low maintenance, just the kind of woman she liked.

"The school called me about my... daughter." Always a complicated sentence. She'd given up explaining the situation to people who didn't need to know. Daughter would do the job for now. "I need Ms. Stein's office. Please." She added the please when she saw the bright green of the guard's eyes. Sexy.

"Yes, ma'am. You'll take the first left and you'll find Ms. Stein's classroom is the second door on the left after that." The guard hesitated. "Sorry to stop you, ma'am. Just doing my job."

There could be flirting here. Could be some kind of connection maybe. And then Alex remembered Libby, why she was here. Shit. She ran off without even thanking the guard.

She found the door fast and burst through it before realizing that the classroom was full of children and she was making quite the entrance. Every eye looked up at her and the back of her neck prickled.

"Ms. Blakely, I presume. Please give me one moment."

At the front of the class stood a slim woman, her silhouette accentuated by a pencil skirt and a tight white blouse opened at the neck. Red beads hung around her neck. Her blonde hair was swept up in a chignon and when she spoke her words had the soft echo of an accent Alex couldn't place. She did know that the tone was dismissive though. Something she didn't like in the slightest.

"Class, please continue. Ms. Benson will be listening from next door to ensure that there's no nonsense. Anyone making noise or not doing their English will be kept inside at break time."

The woman stood for a second as though daring a child to argue with her and Alex had the sudden urge to stick her tongue out at her. So up herself. So coiffed. So perfect. So strict and boring and...

"Come with me, Ms. Blakely."

Alex found herself trailing after the woman feeling for all the world that she was five years old again. They walked a few doors down to a classroom that was empty except for one person. Libby.

Practically smashing open the door, Alex ran in. Libby's face was streaked with dirt and the dress she'd chosen so carefully was torn and stained.

"Darling, what happened?" Alex said, clasping Libby's shoulders and kissing her forehead.

"Olivia got into a fight," said the accented voice from behind. "If you'll please take a seat, Ms. Blakely."

"A fight? What—"

"A seat please, Ms. Blakely."

Alex dragged a chair closer to Libby's and put her hand on the child's arm as she sat down. Ms. Stein stood, arms crossed.

"Are you alright?"

Libby nodded and Alex's heart lifted just a little.

"Now, there was an incident in the playground at lunchtime and Olivia got into a fight with another student. Olivia, would you like to tell us what happened?"

Libby shrugged. "Nothing."

"Olivia, if you choose not to tell the truth then be aware that there will be a punishment. You will go home tonight with a hundred lines to write."

"A hundred lines?" Alex said. "What is this, nineteen-fifty? Who the hell gives lines anymore?"

"I'll ask you to mind your language." Ms. Stein's lips were

pressed together so that they were almost white and Alex desperately wanted to slap her. "Now, Olivia. What happened?"

"I got in a fight with Jayden."

"Did he hurt you?" Alex asked, frantically looking for signs of blood.

"No," said Libby. "I pushed him and then I punched him."

"Did you start this fight, Olivia?" asked Ms. Stein.

"No. Jayden said my dress was stupid so I pushed him and then I punched him."

"I see. Olivia, we had already discussed the rules of the playground."

Libby nodded and looked so sad that Alex wanted to take her in her arms. Instead, she rounded on the teacher. "What the hell kind of place is this that lets kids fight in the playground?" she said. "I thought you were supposed to be responsible for them. Too busy drinking coffee and handing out lines for homework, were you?"

Green eyes flashed onto her face and Alex felt blood rushing to her cheeks as Ms. Stein gave her a withering glance. She shut her mouth feeling like she'd been slapped herself, and Ms. Stein turned her attention back to Libby.

"You will need to apologize to Jayden, write a letter of apology to Jayden's mother, and spend the rest of the day at home thinking about what you've done. You will also need to apologize to your own mother for taking her away from her work and making her come down to the school to pick you up."

Libby's lip was trembling. But she nodded. "Sorry, Alex," she said.

Alex saw Ms. Stein's eyebrows raise as Libby used her first name. Obviously, she didn't approve. But what the hell else was Libby supposed to call her? Or maybe she actually thought she was Libby's mother. But she didn't have a chance to correct her, Ms. Stein was already talking again.

"And you, Ms. Blakely. I would recommend a strong talking to about solving problems with violence. And perhaps, in the future, it would be better to send Olivia to school in more appropriate clothing."

Red mist appeared in front of her eyes. She'd been here before, had spent so many hours sitting in front of disappointed teachers that she'd almost forgotten that she was an adult now, that she didn't need to be patronized or lectured. It was only when Libby gave a small, hiccuping sob that Alex came to her senses.

"Stop calling her Olivia!" She said, struggling out of the chair. "Everyone calls her Libby, as you'd know if you'd ever got off your high horse to actually damn well ask her."

"Ms. Blakely, language, please."

"No, don't 'language, please' me. You criticize Libby for defending herself against some kid's cruel comment, you don't even bother to learn her name properly, and she gets into a fight in your school-yard because she's not being supervised properly, and suddenly all this is my fault because I let her wear a dress to school?"

"Ms. Blakely—"

"No, I won't have this. It's her first day here and already you're letting her be bullied. Well, not on my watch. Libby, get up." Alex held out her hand and Libby stumbled out of her chair and came to take it. "We're out of here."

"But..." Libby said.

"But nothing. You don't have to come back to this horrible place."

"I only excluded Olivia for the afternoon," Ms. Stein said, a red flush appearing on her cheeks and a strand of blonde hair escaping from her chignon now.

"Well, I'm excluding her for the whole rest of the year," Alex spat. "There's no way in hell that my kid's coming here. Not with some witch like you as a teacher. Come on, Libby."

"Ms. Blakely, you are legally required to keep Olivia in school."

Alex said nothing, simply turning slowly and glaring at the teacher. There was a moment there as electricity crackled between them, as her skin prickled into goosebumps, when she knew that she was close to crossing a line. What line, she wasn't sure. She just knew that there was a line right there and she was way too close to it. Her hands itched and she could see herself slapping the woman.

Libby tugged at her hand and the moment was gone, broken.

Without another word, Alex pulled Libby out of the classroom and marched her down the corridor.

So much for public school.

CHAPTER SIX

The bar was heaving with the post-work crowd and Kat seriously regretted letting Fran talk her into this. She pushed her way over until she saw Fran waving.

"Really? After-work drinks? This isn't a teacher thing, you know," she said as she dropped her bag and sat down. "We're too busy marking homework to do this."

"You have homework to mark after the first day? What kind of witch are you?" Fran asked, pushing a glass of white wine her way.

"You know, you're not the first person today to call me a witch."

"I'm the only person you love that calls you witch," Fran said. "Now, have some wine and relax. You deserve it. I know this isn't a regular thing, but I think I get to treat you to a glass or two after your first day back."

"One glass."

"We'll see." Fran grinned. "So, how was it?"

Kat rolled her eyes. "You know, same as ever. Chaos, but the fun kind of chaos where you forget to go to the bathroom for six hours at a stretch. The new kids are a good bunch, high standard too, I've only got two below average readers in the group, which is some kind of miracle, I'm sure."

"I'll take it that day one was a success then."

Kat pulled a face. "Well, there was one thing."

"Spill it!"

"Eugh. Okay, so there was this girl in my class."

"Was? As in past tense?"

"Hold up, let me explain. This girl, Olivia. A very pleasant child, I have to say. Generally polite, pretty little thing, smart as well, reading and math both way above her age standard. But..."

"Parents," Fran said immediately. "That can be the only thing wrong with a kid like that. Who was it, mother or father?"

"Mother. First of all, not only does she send the kid to school in a yellow, designer-label dress, but Olivia also calls her mommy by her first name."

"No shit?"

"Seriously. And when Olivia gets into the inevitable fight in the playground over this stupid dress and I have the parent called in, mom throws a fit and pulls the kid out of school entirely. Which is why we're discussing Olivia in past tense, since she's apparently no longer in my class, or even the school."

"Wow. You know, some people really shouldn't have kids."

"I don't know about that," Kat said. "I do know that some people don't have the first clue how to raise a kid. I mean, really, who does that? Any of it? I feel sorry for the kid."

She took a gulp of wine and as she closed her eyes she could see Libby's mother, her dark blue eyes flashing with anger, her dark hair spiky and stuck up showing off her angular face and high cheekbones. Those yoga pants she'd been wearing, and the cropped t-shirt that showed off a flat, tanned stomach. Really. Even her clothes were inappropriate.

"You can't save them all, Kat, you know that. If this kid's mom doesn't want them in school then I guess there's not much you can do about it."

"At least I won't have to be dealing with her for the rest of the school year," Kat said. "The mom, not the kid. I wouldn't fancy daily visits from a woman like that."

"What about daily visits from any of the other single moms?" Fran asked with a gleam in her eye.

"No!" said Kat immediately. "This is school, not a dating pool.

Not that I'm ready to be jumping into any pools at all yet."

"Gotta get back on the horse, Kat."

"Again, not the first person to tell me that today."

Before Fran could say anything, Kat's mobile started to buzz. It vibrated on the table, the contact name large and white and easy to read. Home, it said. Home because that number had once been home. Not a place, a person. Jen had been her home, wherever she was, Kat had said as much in her wedding vows, and had meant it. Except now Jen wasn't home. Jen was... nothing.

She threw back the rest of her wine in one gulp and picked up the phone. She was damned if she was going to run away from this. Besides, there was always the small chance, the small hope, that Jen wanted... More. That she wanted to apologize, that she'd come to her senses, that...

"Hello."

"Kat, it's me." As if she wouldn't recognize the voice. "Listen, just real fast, you don't know where my passport is, do you?"

"Why would I know that?" She desperately wanted to be angry but couldn't find it in herself. The only thing she could feel was hurt.

"Because the last time I saw it was when we took that break to Montreal and now I can't find the damn thing anywhere."

Ah, Montreal. The last weekend they'd spent away together. The weekend that Kat had thought would save their marriage, could save their marriage. A weekend that they should have spent in bed. A weekend that they spent shouting and arguing and crying. The weekend that Jen had finally told her about Denise. About the woman she'd been cheating with for months.

"I don't have it," Kat said. She paused not wanting to say more but then wasn't able to help herself. She was a teacher, it was in her blood to give advice. "Why don't you just apply for a new one?"

"Because Denise and I are heading down to Mexico to do some kite-surfing tomorrow night and I don't have time," Jen said sharply. "Anyway, I was just checking. Thanks."

She hung up the phone and Kat just stared at her mobile for

a moment. Kite-surfing. She didn't even know what that was. It sounded... exciting, she supposed. The kind of excitement that Jen had been looking for and she hadn't been able to provide. Boring Kat with her home decorating and teaching and baby-fever.

"You know, you really need to change that contact name in your phone," Fran said.

Kat nodded slowly. "Yeah, yeah, I do." She swallowed. "Um, listen, this was a nice idea. It really was. And thank you. But I really do want to get back now. I have some lesson prep to do and I could use a good night's sleep."

"Sure thing," Fran said. "I already got the check. Come on, let's go."

And once again she thanked her lucky stars for a friend as understanding as Fran. Someone who knew that after a conversation with her ex all she really wanted to do was have a quiet cry in her bedroom for an hour or so.

Finger on the mouse button, Kat took a solid deep breath before she clicked on the 'results' icon. There was a nail-biting pause and then up popped a list of the best career choices she was suited for based on the online test she'd just taken.

Teacher.

Fantastic. Well, at least she knew that the test worked.

Financial advisor came a close second and she didn't even know what that was, followed by corporate trainer. Interesting, Trisha had mentioned that one. The list just got ridiculous after that. But at least there were options.

Idly, she wondered what Olivia's mother did. What kind of job could the woman have that allowed her to show up in yoga pants and a t-shirt? Maybe she was some kind of fitness instructor. That would explain the flat stomach, she supposed. Given the name-tag on the designer dress Olivia had been wearing, fitness instructors got paid a hell of a lot more than elementary school teachers.

She put her hand over her own stomach. How would it compare to Ms. Blakely's? Just a thought. Just... She blinked and shook her head. She needed sleep. After not sleeping the night before and that stupid phone call from Jen, she really needed to go to bed.

She closed down her laptop and crawled into bed.

There were so many things she needed.

A new career. A bunch of money. A place of her own. A bed that she owned rather than borrowed. A car that wasn't on the verge of falling apart. A new outfit or two.

A new love.

She shook her head again. That had come out of nowhere. She wasn't ready for that yet. She really wasn't. But she missed cuddling up in bed next to someone. She missed having warmth there, missed having someone to laugh at her jokes and mistakes, someone to tell her deepest thoughts and desires and fears to.

What a day. There were large parts of it that she'd really rather forget. Not least the fact that she'd finally found out what kite-surfing was and even the idea of it had terrified her. Maybe Jen had been right. Maybe she was boring.

On the bright side, at least she'd never have to see Olivia's mother again. So the day wasn't a complete write-off.

She switched off the light and closed her eyes. But her dreams, when they came, were very, very confusing ones. Kite-surfing, her arms around the slim waist of an instructor, the waves crashing around her, the salt air sharp on her face. And when the instructor turned around... bright blue eyes and spiky dark hair and an irritated look of anger on her face. Olivia Blakely's mother.

CHAPTER SEVEN

Libby was the ultimate in giving the cold shoulder. Something that always reminded Alex of her sister. Claire had been able to go for days without speaking to Alex over some tiny slight, whereas Alex would break her own vow of silence after seconds. And the trait was just as irritating in Claire's daughter as it had been in her mother.

"Libby, are you going to talk to me?" Alex said as she pulled the car into the driveway.

In answer, Libby unclasped her own seatbelt and started opening the door before Alex had even come to a full stop. She slammed on the brakes. Libby didn't seem to notice. The kid climbed out of the car and went to sit on the front step.

Alex parked properly and took a second to collect herself.

"She's a kid. A little kid. She's already hurt. You don't get to be angry with her." She whispered the words to herself, trying to calm her irritation. Only then did she get out of the car.

"Libby, if you're mad or upset about something, we really need to talk about it."

Libby glared at her, a world of anger on her little face.

"Remember what Dr. Sarah said after mommy's accident? That keeping things inside isn't good. It makes us..." She trailed off, waiting for Libby to finish the sentence.

"Explode," Libby spat.

Alex bit her lip to stop herself laughing. Taking Libby to see a child psychologist after Claire's death was certainly one of the few things that she'd actually done right. "That's right," she said. "So, I'm gonna unlock the door and then I need you to talk to me."

Libby crossed her arms and pouted and Alex opened the door and dropped her purse inside before holding the door so Libby could go in. When the door was closed again, Alex leaned up against it.

"So?"

For a second she thought that Libby wasn't going to respond at all. Maybe she didn't even know why she was mad. Maybe it was just the stress of the day that was making her upset. Maybe she was mad at herself for being thrown out of school. Maybe she was mad at whatever the kid's name was that she hit. Maybe she was mad at Alex for letting her wear that damn yellow dress.

"I hate you."

Alex's mouth dropped open for a second and she hurriedly closed it again. "What?"

"I hate you. I hate this house. I hate this car. I hate this dress. And I hate you." Libby punctuated this with a couple of foot stamps.

"Okay," Alex said slowly. Turn it around, she told herself. At least the kid was talking. Just turn it around. "Is there anything that you like?"

"I like Ms. Stein."

Libby flounced up the stairs and slammed her bedroom door, leaving Alex open-mouthed again at the bottom of the stairs. What in the hell?

With a sigh, she took herself to the kitchen. She studiously ignored the bottle of white wine in the fridge and poured herself an orange juice. Maybe she'd give things a little time to calm down. Give Libby time to figure out what she wanted, what she was mad about. Because the kid obviously had no idea.

Why would any kid love a teacher like that? Alex shuddered in remembered pain. Teachers that would only accept homework if the date was written in a certain way, that would only let you sit in alphabetical order. She had a harsh memory of a math teacher that would only accept papers that had zero mistakes, so an errant mark from a pen meant starting over again from the beginning.

Yes, she had Ms. Stein's number. And she was glad that she'd done what she'd done. Alright, she could have been slightly less dramatic about it. But getting Libby out of that woman's classroom was smart. Libby needed room to grow, a place to be herself, somewhere to play and be calm and learn at her own pace.

She didn't need to be under the thumb of some elementary school dictator.

Christ. Life used to be so much easier.

Life used to be made up of three problems. Where to sleep for the night, how to get enough cash to move on to the next place she wanted to go, and who to sleep with for the night. Evie had been her latest partner in crime, but even that had been slowly winding its way down.

No commitments, that had been the plan. That had always been the plan. She'd seen amazing things, done amazing things, and the only thing she ever wanted was the next amazing thing. Sunsets on Thai beaches, breakfasts in Cambodian villages, nights spent under Turkish stars. Only ever owning what would fit inside her backpack. That was it.

And now she owned a house.

Claire's money had bought it, which made it seem less her own. But it was Alex's name on the deed.

Suddenly, she felt very, very lonely.

Time for emergency procedures.

She opened up the freezer and pulled out a bag of dinosaur chicken nuggets, arranged a handful on a plate, and stuck it in the microwave. Libby wouldn't be able to resist. The world was full of problems. Her world was full of problems. She had to tackle them one at a time. And this thing with Libby was first in line.

"Can I come in?"

"No."

Alex grinned and cracked the door just enough to wave the plate of dinosaur nuggets through. "Can I come in now?"

Silence. Then: "Yes."

With a sigh of relief, she pushed open the door. Libby was sitting on the floor, her back against her bed, so Alex joined her there, passing over the plate of nuggets.

"Alright, kiddo, why don't we talk about what's going on here?"

"'kay," Libby said, her mouth full of nugget.

The kid was easy to please, Alex gave her that. "So, want to tell me why you're so mad?"

"Because of school."

Not helpful. "Um, which part of school made you mad?"

"You."

Alex could see this conversation devolving rapidly. "Right. Okay, let's start over." She clung onto the one piece of info that she had. "You love Ms. Stein?"

Libby nodded. "She's great. She gave us lots of things to do and told us all the rules and there's stickers if we do things good and she says 'break time' instead of 'recess' and..."

"But she's so strict," Alex said. "Wouldn't you like a nicer teacher? One who's friendlier?"

"Nope," Libby said. "I like this one. Anyway, she's pretty."

It took a second for that to register. And a longer second for Alex to register that she actually agreed with the kid. Ms. Stein was pretty, she guessed. Not that that was important.

"She doesn't even call you by your right name," Alex said, knowing that she was being petty, that she was trying to persuade Libby not to like the woman.

Libby just shrugged. "It's okay when she does it."

"Okay. So you're mad because...?" She had a feeling she knew what was going to happen now.

"Because you told Ms. Stein that I couldn't go back to school. And I want to. I like it there. There's a playground and a school bus and there's no uniform and I like Ms. Stein. And now I'll never, never go there again and..." Libby's lip was wobbling and tears were already collecting.

"Hold up there, kiddo. You're going to choke on your nuggets. You're saying that you want to go to this school? You want to be in that class?"

Libby nodded, her cheeks flushed and a tear escaping from the corner of one eye. Alex rubbed her face with her hands. Shit.

"You absolutely sure?"

Libby nodded again and her face was starting to crumple and Alex put her arm around her, disregarding the plate of dino nuggets that slid onto the floor. Then Libby was sobbing and Alex was hating what she was about to do. But it wasn't like she had a choice. If this was what the kid wanted, then this had to be it, didn't it?

"Okay, then we can go back tomorrow morning."

"You mean it?" Libby pulled back.

Alex sighed and nodded. "But I'll have to take you in the car tomorrow. I guess I'll have some explaining to do. You can take the bus again on Monday, okay?"

Libby nodded happily and picked up a nugget of the carpet. Alex picked up the one next to it and took a bite. Not bad. She'd eaten worse. Not as bad as the crow she was going to have to eat in the morning in front of fucking Ms. Stein.

"Lib?"

"Yeah?" The word was muffled by dino nugget.

"You don't really hate me, do you?"

There was a pause and a sniff. "No. Not today."

Not today.

Well, it was a start, she supposed.

How the hell had a seven year old made her life so damn complicated, so hard? And as of tomorrow, life was about to be even harder. Because in the morning she was going to have some serious apologizing to do.

"Give me another nugget, Libby. I need one."

Libby handed over a nugget and Alex bit it in half. It would pair quite nicely with the white wine in the fridge, she decided.

CHAPTER EIGHT

"Verdammte scheisse."
Kat kicked the wheel of the car, which achieved exactly nothing.

"I'd have gone with 'fucking piece of shit' myself," Fran said, tossing her own keys in the air. "But that's just me."

"Means pretty much the same," Kat said.

"And yet it sounds so much... worse in German," said Fran. "So, what's the plan here?"

Kat wanted to rub her eyes but since this was the one morning when she'd actually made an effort and put on some makeup, she restrained herself. The plan? Like there was a plan. The car was dead in the water, if it could be fixed it was probably going to cost a bomb. If it couldn't be fixed, she'd have to get a new car which would definitely cost a bomb.

Either way, her savings had been cut back by at least a third. Bringing that scary 'you're too broke to eat' deadline even closer.

There was public transport in Germany. She could remember as a kid taking the tram to school with her friends, the bell dinging at different stops. In America, of course, a car was a necessity, not a luxury. She couldn't even remember if her parents had owned a car before they'd emigrated.

"Yo! Hey! Little miss thing!"

Kat blinked and shook herself out of her daydream. Going

back to Germany wasn't plan B. It wasn't plan C or D either. It hovered somewhere around plan M. Speaking of plans, the car, right. "Okay, the plan is that you're going to drive me to school." Leaving a class of seven-year-olds to their own devices was not a good plan.

"Short and sweet, I like it. Got a plan for the car?" Fran asked.

"Nope," Kat said as she climbed into Fran's passenger seat. "Could burn it, I suppose."

"Environmental regulations," Fran said. "We could pimp out the inside and rent it as an Air BnB?"

Kat laughed, but it was half-hearted. This hadn't been the start to her morning that she needed. And as much as she knew she shouldn't sweat the small stuff, knew that she should accept the things she couldn't control, her life had gotten a whole lot worse in the space of the last few minutes. And, as it always had for the last few months, it all came down to money.

Things weren't about to get much better either. As Fran screeched up in front of the school, Kat reached down to pick up her bag and lunch-box and realized that they were all still in her own car.

"What's the problem?" Fran asked.

"Nothing," said Kat. No lunch today then. "Thanks for the ride."

"Need me to pick you up?" Fran asked. "It's really not a problem."

She wanted to say no but it was too far to walk and she really couldn't afford the cab. She hated to make Fran get off work early, even though Fran always said it wasn't an issue. Then she remembered something.

"That'd be great," she said, feeling slightly less guilty. "I won't be done until at least five though, there's some kind of parent representative meeting after school."

"Perfect-o," Fran said. Her blonde hair was gleaming and she shot Kat a wink. "I'll be here. In the meantime, turn that frown upside down and go make today a better day than it started."

That optimism again. But this time Kat gave a real smile. She pressed Fran's hand before she got out of the car.

"Lucas Kalnik, put that book down immediately. And Daniel Lewis, if I see you so much as touch Adele again you'll be inside for both break times and at lunch."

The shrieking and shouting continued and Kat knew that she was being drowned out, that she was being overwhelmed. Her head throbbed with pain. She moved so that she was standing in front of the whiteboard.

"Class, sit down this minute!"

Her voice was ten decibels louder than it needed to be and had climbed at least an octave. But it worked. A sudden silence descended in the room and then there was a shuffling of chairs as the kids finally settled down. Jesus. What a morning. It must be a full moon tonight, she figured, the kids were just way too full of beans.

"Take out your reading books and read at your own desks for fifteen minutes. Anyone who isn't reading or who makes a sound will be inside all day with no break times."

A muffled groan and then rustling as the children found their books and then the creak of the classroom door opening. Kat turned to see a small figure in the doorway.

Olivia Blakely, dressed today in jeans and a simple striped t-shirt, was standing there, her face anxious but excited. And hovering behind her was her mother. Seriously. Could her day get any worse? Kat briefly considered just jumping out of the window right now. But they were only on the first floor. Knowing her luck she'd get nothing more than two broken legs and a boat-load of medical bills.

"Olivia," she said, gravely. "Why don't you take a seat at your desk? We're doing quiet reading time."

The anxiety on Libby's face disappeared immediately, and with a beaming grin she trotted off to her desk in the first row. Kat surveyed the classroom, saw everyone was doing as they were supposed to, and nodded at Olivia's mother.

"Let's talk out here," she said, quietly and calmly, as she ushered Ms. Blakely out into the corridor.

She closed the classroom door, still able to see what was happening inside through the glass pane. Little pitchers had big ears, as her mother had used to say, and she didn't want the children overhearing whatever the hell was about to happen.

"So, Ms. Blakely?" She wasn't about to make this easy. It was obvious what had happened. The woman had come to her senses and realized she couldn't keep a child at home all day.

To give the woman credit, she had the balls to look her in the eye. Kat noticed how blue those eyes were, a deep, deep blue, almost indigo.

"I owe you an apology. I was too hasty yesterday."

"I see." Still not going to make things easy. She wasn't about to let the woman think that she was in control of the situation, that Kat could be walked over and yelled at or anything else.

Now Ms. Blakely did look down, her feet shifted uncomfortably, like a small child in trouble. "The truth of the matter is that Libby likes you. She likes being in your class, and she desperately wanted to come back."

A little spark of happiness lit inside Kat. "That's sweet."

Ms. Blakely shrugged and looked up again. "I don't agree with your teaching methods. From what I've seen, you're strict and too hard on the kids. But this isn't about me, it's about Libby. And if this is what she wants, then I'll do anything in my power to get it for her. So who do I need to speak to? The principal? The school board?"

There was a brute honesty there. It was clear that the woman loved her daughter and was willing to do the right thing by her. All of which was great. There was still one more thing though.

"The only person you need to speak to about getting Olivia back in my class is me," she said. Thank God she hadn't had time to go and explain things to the principal yet.

"Okay, then what do I have to say to convince you?" Those blue eyes were burning and Kat suppressed a shiver.

"It's clear to me that you and I don't see eye to eye about child-rearing," Kat said. "But I think we can come to an agreement. I won't interfere with your parenting if you don't interfere with my teaching. If we agree on this, then I have no problem having your daughter in my class."

Kat had no choice but to have Olivia in her class, but Ms. Blakely didn't know that. And play her cards right and she could avoid having to deal with an irate Ms. Blakely every time things weren't perfect with Olivia.

"Fine."

Kat raised her eyebrows. That easy, huh? Maybe she should argue with parents more often. "In that case, I shall see you at the parents' meeting this afternoon."

"Parents meeting?" Ms. Blakely said.

"It starts at four."

The woman nodded and without saying anything further walked away. Kat watched her. She was still wearing yoga pants. They still curved around her backside like they were molded to it. Kat felt a burst of heat. The same burst of heat she used to feel about seeing any attractive woman. One that she hadn't felt for months now.

It was nothing personal, of course. Ms. Blakely was going to be trouble no matter what they had agreed on, Kat could always tell. But maybe her sex drive was starting to come back. Maybe she was going to recover from Jen. It was not an unpleasant thought. Uncomfortable, yes. She hadn't slept with a woman other than her wife for years. But not unpleasant. A sign that she wasn't as broken as she thought maybe.

And not something she should be thinking about with a class full of second graders to take care of.

She opened the classroom door and all was quiet, heads bent over books. She walked to the whiteboard. Even her incipient headache was starting to ease. And, she suddenly remembered, there was a handful of change in her desk drawer that would be more than enough to get a salad for lunch.

In fact, the only dark spot she could see in the rest of her day was having to see that damn woman again at the parents' meeting.

CHAPTER NINE

Libby flew at Alex, gripping her tight around the legs until she picked her up and swung her around.

"How was your day, sweetie?"

"Perfect. Amazing. And I love you 'cos now I'm in Ms. Stein's class again. And Ms. Stein says we have to tell the truth always and to use our words. So that's what I'm doing."

Alex grinned. Libby was a chatterbox, always had been. But she was glad that at least she'd made somebody happy. Okay, apologizing to that stupid teacher hadn't been the easiest thing she'd ever done, but Libby was smiling again and that was what mattered.

And Ms. Stein had been right about one thing. They just had to stay out of each other's way. Which shouldn't exactly be difficult. Libby wanted to take the bus, which meant no morning drop offs. So exactly how often would she need to see the witch?

"Can we go get ice cream now?" Libby was tugging at her arm.

Okay, well, there was right now, of course. But this had to be an exception. "Not now, kiddo."

"Why? Is it 'cos ice cream's bad for you. I know that but sometimes you can like things that are bad for you anyway."

Alex had a flashback to pretty much every woman she'd ever dated. Talk about liking something that was bad for you. Which led to her thinking about Libby dating, and then... Jesus. Okay. Libby was seven, no need to deal with the hell of dating yet.

"Can we get ice cream then?" Libby asked again.

"Nope," Alex said. "I gotta go to a parent representative meeting."

"What's that?"

She shrugged. "Beats me. I'll tell you when I get out. But while I'm there you're supposed to go to the gym and there's going to be games and other kids to play with until all the parents are done."

"You're not a parent," Libby said, eyes narrowing.

Alex swallowed. "Not exactly."

"So you don't have to go. So we can get ice cream."

Alex wondered who had gone to these meetings at Libby's old school. She didn't see Claire taking time off work to go. The nanny maybe. "We'll get ice cream after, promise. Plus, you get extra play time with your friends instead of going home with boring old me."

"You're not boring," Libby said grinning.

Not old either, thought Alex, even though I feel like I'm sixty sometimes.

She kind of wished she still had her college hip flask. She'd kill for a drink right now. Though there was probably some kind of law against drinking in an elementary school. There had to be, right? Alex crept along the corridor, looking for the sign saying that she was in the right place. And when she finally found it, she wanted a drink more than ever.

She's nothing to be afraid of, she told herself. She's a stupid teacher. It wasn't like Ms. Stein held any kind of authority over her, after all. But it was some kind of gut reaction. The woman pissed her off for all kinds of reasons. Not least because she couldn't be bothered to even learn Libby's name properly.

Olivia, as Libby often pointed out, sounded like the name of one of those stupid American Girl Dolls. And Libby hated dolls. Always had. One of the many things that Alex liked about her.

Shit. Okay, she needed to do this. She had no idea what she was getting into or even really why she was there except that it was the right thing to do and people were supposed to go to these things.

She straightened herself up, held her chin up high and pushed the door open. Far too hard, as it turned out, meaning that she stumbled and half-fell into the classroom.

"Sorry, sorry," she said, feeling blood rushing to her cheeks.

"Not a problem, we were just getting started."

Alex took a deep breath and raised her head. There were four other women in the room. None of whom were Ms. Stein.

"Um, this is for Ms. Stein's class, right?" she asked.

"Yes," said the only blonde, who was sitting slightly apart from the others like she might be in charge. "Ms. Stein has been delayed but will be joining us shortly. In the meantime, I suggest we get this thing started."

Alex slipped into a chair next to a dark-haired woman who had something that looked like it might be baby sick on her shoulder. "Shouldn't we wait for everyone else?"

The blonde woman snorted. "Everyone else? The sensible parents keep the hell away from meetings like this one. They save themselves for the important things, like PTA and parent-teacher conferences. Let me guess, you're all parents with kids new to the school?"

Alex nodded and so did everyone else. Sensible parents kept away from meetings like this? Meetings like what? If this wasn't PTA or a parent-teacher conference then what the hell was it? And why was she here? She glanced at the door. But the blonde was already starting to speak again. Too late to run away, she guessed.

"The sooner we get this done, the sooner we can all get out of here."

Alex raised her hand. It was instinctual. They were in a classroom. Some long-buried sense of what was supposed to happen in places like this stirred within her. "Um, the sooner we get what done?"

"Elect the parent representative," the blonde said. "So I suggest we introduce ourselves. I'm Sandy Higgs, and I'm going to go ahead and take myself out of the running here. I'm already parent representative for my older son's class, so obviously I can't do both."

One by one the women introduced themselves, giving their full names, and right up until her turn Alex was still trying to figure out just what the hell a parent representative was.

"Alex Blakely," she said when she was the only one who hadn't spoken. "And—"

"There'll be time for questions later," the blonde said. The other three women were shifting uncomfortably in their chairs like they knew they'd already made a huge mistake, other than the woman sitting next to Alex who was wide-eyed and looked like she hadn't slept for weeks. "So, do we have any volunteers for the position?"

The silence that greeted the question was almost tangible. Alex was beginning to think that she really needed to make friends with another parent. Maybe if she had had inside information she'd know what she was doing here. Hell, she'd know not to come in the first place.

Still silence.

Jesus, this was ridiculous.

Nobody could volunteer for something if they didn't know what the hell it was.

Running out of patience, Alex stuck her hand up in the air again. "Hey, I—"

"Excellent, thank you, Ms. Blakely. I'll get your information to Ms. Stein as soon as she arrives," said the blonde.

Woah. Hold on here. "No, wait, hey, I just wanted to know what the hell a parent representative is supposed to be, that's all," Alex said quickly.

The blonde sniffed. "A parent rep takes care of all the extra things that the class teacher can't. For example, you'll organize bake sales and fund-raising activities, perhaps set up a car pool system or an emergency calling circle for circumstances that might require it. In short, you'll take responsibility for things connected to the class, but not directly connected to teaching."

Responsibility. Not the word that Alex wanted to hear.

"Oh no," she said. "I can't—"

"Well, I can't do it," chipped in the mother opposite Alex. "I've got a full time job. I'm only here because I didn't know how unimportant this was going to be."

"I work too," said the mother next to her.

Which left Alex and the sleep-starved woman next to her. Alex closed her eyes. "I can't do this," she said.

"Do you work?" asked the blonde.

"No," Alex said. "But I've got tattoos!"

The blonde just stared at her and Alex knew it had been a stupid thing to say but it had been the first thing that popped into her head. She did have tattoos. Surely responsible parent representatives didn't have tattoos. Did they?

"I guess..." Started the mother next to Alex.

She didn't finish the sentence, catching sight of the baby sick on her shoulder and reaching for a tissue to wipe it down. And Alex knew she couldn't let this one go. The woman obviously had at least a second grader and a baby. She barely knew her own name and looked more exhausted than Alex had ever seen someone look and still be able to speak.

For fuck's sake.

"Fine, I'll do it."

The door opened just as the blonde was standing up telling them all that they could make their longed-for escape. Alex looked at the ground. There could only be one person that walked into a classroom like they owned it.

"Ah, Ms. Stein," the blonde said with a smile. "I'd like you to meet your new second grade parent representative. Ms. Blakely, have you met Ms. Stein?"

Alex blew out a breath. "Yes," she said tiredly. "Yes, I have."

CHAPTER TEN

Kat's heart sank like a stone in water. This was so not what she needed. But she was used to hiding her disappointment, to not showing her real emotions on her face. So she forced herself to smile.

"Excellent. Thank you, Ms. Higgs, I see you've been efficient. If there's nothing else you need from me…?"

She looked around the room but the other mothers were already gathering their things. Only Olivia's mother was sitting and waiting, watching, her face sulky looking now. Kat bit her tongue. At a guess, Ms. Blakely had been a poor student herself and probably a rebellious one. Someone that still held some foolish ideas about authority and squirmed under its gaze.

"Thank you for volunteering, Ms. Blakely."

Why had she volunteered? Surely this wasn't something the woman wanted to do? And it went against everything they'd talked about only this morning. Staying out of each other's way, that was. Kat felt a prickling of anger. The woman just couldn't stop herself interfering, could she?

"I didn't exactly volunteer."

"Oh, well, thank you for doing the job anyway, I suppose. Parent rep is important, particularly to us teachers. Having another adult we can count on to take some of the responsibilities off our shoulders is a blessing."

Ms. Blakely looked down at her desk and for a second Kat

could see her as the scowling teenager she must once have been. Her t-shirt was slashed across the neck, a style that was fashionable but that Kat hated. Why make your clothes look as though they were old and torn? The smooth bumps of the woman's collarbone were visible, a shining trail leading downwards.

Kat coughed. The lustful feelings had taken her by surprise again. She really was coming back into her own. Maybe Fran was right, maybe it was time to start thinking about dating again.

"So, I have here a list of your main responsibilities," she said briskly, handing over a sheet of paper. "If you'll just give me your contact information I'll make sure that you get a list of the email addresses and phone numbers of the other parents so that you can coordinate activities and the like."

"Activities?" croaked Ms. Blakely. She was starting to look a little pale.

Kat flashed her a grim smile. Parent reps had their fair share of work to do. She guessed that Ms. Blakely hadn't put much thought into that when she'd agreed to do the job. "Activities," she echoed. "Your first big responsibility is going to be the bake sale. That's two weeks from now. It's an important fundraiser for our School in Nature trip, so it's important that we make as much as possible."

"School in Nature?"

Kat had to force herself not to roll her eyes. Honestly, had the woman no clue about school, about what happened during the school year? There were brochures, she herself had sent a newsletter out at the beginning of term. Something that Ms. Blakely obviously hadn't read. She gritted her teeth.

"I'll ensure that you get more information about that," she said. "In the meantime, if you have any questions...?" The woman was still staring down at the paper she'd been given. "No? Then I should let you get back to Olivia. Many thanks, Ms. Blakely."

She looked up then, deep blue eyes glittering. Again, Kat was struck by how almost purple they were. "If we're going to be working together, you should call me Alex."

Kat stared at her for just one second. Working together. It suddenly struck her that they wouldn't be working together. There was no way Alex Blakely could turn her hippie ways into anything efficient enough to run a bake sale. Which meant that the work would fall onto Kat's shoulders instead.

She took a deep breath. "If you don't mind, I prefer to keep things formal."

There was a heartbeat of silence and she saw the look of... disgust maybe, dislike definitely, flash across the woman's face. But she held her own, kept eye contact. Ms. Blakely was going to cost her plenty of time and more than enough stress, she wasn't going to be outdone by some hippie in yoga pants that thought her daughter was old enough to call her by her first name.

"Sure," Ms. Blakely said finally.

Kat gave her a brief nod and then walked out of the classroom, still seething at the thought of all the extra work she'd need to do to make up for what the woman obviously lacked.

Kicking off her shoes at the end of the day and stretching out on Fran's deep couch was one of the little luxuries that Kat enjoyed most. It was free, which meant it had a lot of appeal. And her aching calf muscles twinged in appreciation as she pulled out her laptop and started responding to parent emails.

It was a half hour of quiet that she desperately needed. Fran's habit was to shower the second she got home, meaning Kat got a little unwinding time too. Which was just as well, since Fran had been bouncing around in the car when she picked Kat up.

"Guess what! Guess what!" she'd chirped.

Kat, still reeling a little from Alex Blakely becoming her damn parent rep hadn't been in the mood. "What?"

Fran pulled a face. "If you're going to be like that, then I won't tell you."

"Fine." Kat slammed the car door and buckled her seat-belt.

"But it's so good!" Fran said.

Kat sighed. Okay, she needed to chill out. Her shitty afternoon wasn't Fran's fault. "Sorry. Crappy mood. My bad. Tell me your exciting news. Don't say you've been promoted again?"

"Not even close," Fran said with a grin. "This is exciting news for you, not for me."

"Um... Cate Blanchett is in town and wants my phone number?" Kat guessed, deciding she might as well play along.

"Psh. Not likely. I'm straight as a die, darling, and if Cate asked me for your phone number even I'd be tempted to give her my own. Try again."

"Uh... You got me a puppy?" Lame guess, but she seriously had no idea at all and was yearning for an early night she was so tired.

"No. Fine. I'll tell you." Fran glanced in the rear-view mirror and changed lanes. "So, you remember I told you about Jackson?"

"Um, flirtatious, nice ass, wears a cologne you hate?" You couldn't be a teacher if you had a bad memory.

"That's the one. Works in HR. Which is the exciting part. I was talking to him today at lunch and..."

"And what?" Fran said, starting to lose patience. Her feet were aching.

"And... The company is looking to hire on a full-time corporate trainer," Fran said.

It took a second, more than a heartbeat, before Kat realized the implications of this. When she did her gut reaction was one of fear. "No," she said quickly. "No, there's no way I'm qualified for something like that."

"You are," Fran said. "You have a teaching qualification. That's all that's required. You've got experience too. The company is going to send the candidate to some special training program for six weeks, so they want someone with teaching experience, but also someone moldable. That makes you perfect."

But all Kat could think about was losing her children. Not seeing gap-toothed smiles every morning. Not eating pudding cups for snack, not drying tears, not...

"Kat, come on. It's a great opportunity, and one that you know about before pretty much anyone else. That could really give you the leg up. The salary will be good, you know that."

The lump in her throat was too big to allow her to speak and she had to swallow twice. Fran was being helpful. Fran was being realistic. Fran was being kind. "Thank you," she said finally. "Just give me a while to digest the news."

Fran frowned but didn't bring up the subject again.

But now, lying on the couch with the sound of the shower in the background, it was all Kat could think about.

Sacrifices had to be made. She knew that. She knew that she couldn't always have what she wanted. Obviously.

Without thinking she logged into her bank account. The number at the top of the page was growing steadily smaller. Add in the cost of car repair and it was going to be smaller still. And she couldn't live with Fran forever.

She'd thought about a second job, working more fast-food shifts maybe. But she was so exhausted at the end of every day, and she still had homework to grade and lessons to plan.

She stared at her bank balance.

Her stomach flipped over. She'd only ever wanted to be a teacher. Nothing else. Couldn't imagine doing anything else.

"An interview isn't a commitment."

She jumped. She hadn't realized that the shower had stopped. Fran was standing in the doorway, wrapped in her robe.

"An interview isn't a commitment. You could go, have a look around, find out more about the job. You might not even get it," Fran said.

She was right. No commitment. Kat took one last look at her bank balance and then nodded. "Okay," she said. "Alright, I'm interested."

CHAPTER ELEVEN

Alex scrolled through the shared spreadsheet. Every box was filled, every parent had taken at least one kind of baked good. She was impressed. Not with herself, setting up a shared spreadsheet and linking all the other parents into it had been easy and taken no more than a couple of minutes. But with the other parents. They all wanted to be involved with the bake sale. It was sweet. She hadn't realized how committed other people could be.

"So, are we doing this?"

She turned around to see Libby wearing a shirt that was ten sizes too big and looked suspiciously familiar. "Did you raid my closet?"

"Ms. Stein says that it's important to cover your clothes when you're going to make a mess because money doesn't grow on trees."

Alex nodded. Fair point, she guessed. "And what makes you think that we're going to be making a mess?"

"Doesn't baking make a mess?"

From what she remembered, no. But frankly, she only had hazy memories of her mother making birthday cakes. Still, better safe than sorry, another saying that she'd bet money Ms. Stein would like.

"Alrighty, go grab the recipes from the printer and then we'll get started."

Libby ran off and Alex stretched and checked the time. Four o'clock on a Sunday afternoon, never her favorite time of the week. The kind of time when she'd rather be sitting at a beach bar with a cocktail in her hand. Or climbing a mountain. Or riding a yak. Or any one of a thousand other things.

"Let's go!" cried Libby from the kitchen.

"Well, what does the recipe say?" she asked through gritted teeth.

"Three tablespoons of flour," Libby read slowly.

Tablespoons. Was that the big spoon or the little one? She could never remember. It was flour, which she guessed was pretty important in a brownie, so she went with the big spoon, but it really was a toss up.

"This is no fun," pouted Libby.

"It's for your bake sale," pointed out Alex. "So you're sticking around kiddo."

"I wanna go watch TV."

"Nope, keep reading."

She threw the flour into the bowl, stirring up a mist of fine white particles. This was not how she's imagined this situation. This was definitely not how she remembered her mother doing things. And this was her third attempt.

The first attempt had been thwarted by a terrific smell that had turned out to be a bad egg. Probably. The second attempt had made it as far as the mixing process, but had then been splattered over the counter and cabinets when she'd apparently turned the mixer on too fast.

"There's just eggs now," Libby said.

Having learned her lesson, Alex broke the eggs into a separate bowl before mixing them in. "So we're done?"

"Finished," Libby said with certainty.

"Sure?"

"Yes."

Alex sighed. "Fine. You can go and watch TV now. Take a snack pack out of the fridge, I'll deal with dinner after the brownies are done."

Libby trotted off quite happily as Alex slid the tray of brownies into the oven.

"They're not supposed to smell like that," Libby said, peering into the pan.

"I don't think they're supposed to look like that either," confessed Alex.

Her heart thudded and she felt vaguely sick. She'd committed to bringing a double batch of brownies to the bake sale and it was almost six and she hadn't accomplished a thing. Who the hell knew that baking was going to be so difficult?

"You tried very hard," Libby said.

Alex put an arm around her. "Thanks, kiddo. But I don't think I tried hard enough."

"Ms. Stein says that we should look for the good things about people, not the bad things."

Alex was growing heartily sick of hearing Ms. Stein's name. On the one hand, she was happy that Libby liked school and her teacher. On the other... she could really do without having to think about the witch of a teacher fifty times a day. She shuddered. What was Ms. Stein going to say about her parent rep turning up to the bake sale empty handed?

"Get your jacket," she said to Libby. "We're going out."

Libby ran off. She could buy brownies, right? That was a thing. Maybe. Or was that cheating? She had no idea what was expected of her. She had a feeling that Ms. Stein was going to frown on store-bought cakes, but she didn't exactly have much choice.

"Where are you guys headed?" Doug wheeled his trash can to the curb just as Libby was climbing into her car seat.

A look of horror crossed his face when Alex told him what they were doing. "Oh no," he said. "No, no, no. Get out of that car and march right into my kitchen. Come on, right now."

Doug's mixer was the most professional looking thing that Alex had ever seen, and she'd worked her share of restaurant jobs. It quietly hummed away as Libby scooped up the last of the trash and put it in the trash can.

"Nice work, Libby," Doug said.

"Ms. Stein says that we have to clean up our own mess."

Alex growled under her breath and Doug raised an eyebrow at her. She shook her head.

"Doug, I'm hungry."

Doug grinned and went to the fridge. "I got some of my special spaghetti left. You want it?"

Libby nodded. Whilst Doug hadn't babysat yet, Alex had made a point of introducing the two, and after Doug had come over for pizza one night, he'd reciprocated with a dish of his famous spaghetti. Which Libby had predictably loved as much as she loved any food that stained or made a mess.

"Why don't you go turn the TV on while I put this in the microwave," Doug said. "Me and Alex can wait for the brownies to be done."

Alex sighed. There was always a little loosening inside her when there was another adult around, a small lightening of the load. She'd learned to appreciate it, to take it whenever she could. And Doug was good with children, he and Libby got on like a house on fire.

"So, Ms. Stein, huh?" he said as soon as Libby was gone.

"If I hear her name one more time tonight, I'll scream."

"Not your favorite person still, I take it?"

"She sets my teeth on edge. Everything about her makes me

want to slap her."

"Compensating for anything there?"

Alex pulled a face at him and he grinned as he pulled out a baking sheet and switched off the mixer.

"She just... She just gets my back up. And Libby thinks the sun shines out of her... behind. God knows why."

"I could take a guess," Doug said. "Why do you hate her so much?"

"Because she's a relic. Like something out of the fifties. I'm surprised she doesn't cane the kids. She has them writing lines, sitting in alphabetical order, the whole nine yards."

"Ah, close to retirement and not willing to deal with new-fangled ways of teaching?"

Alex rolled her eyes. "Not even. She's my age. Built like some kind of super model and is so well-put-together it makes you want to spread mud on her shirt just to give you something to look at." She bit down on her tongue. She hadn't meant to say that, didn't even know where it came from.

Doug chose to ignore it. "But Libby likes her. What about the other kids?"

"They all adore her," Alex said. "Which kind of makes it worse." She sighed. "They're only in second grade."

A waft of heat came as Doug opened the oven door and slid the brownies in. He wiped his hands on a cloth. "It's a psychological fact that children like discipline," he said. He held up a hand to stop Alex interrupting him. "I don't mean they like being spanked. I mean they like having clear rules and limits, it helps them understand a world that can be overwhelming. It's good for them."

"But what about play and imagination and making mistakes and your own decisions and everything else?" Alex asked.

Doug scratched his nose. "Libby gets all those things from you, doesn't she?"

"Sure, but—"

"Then don't worry," Doug said. "Life is all about balance. If this woman is a good teacher, and the kids like her, and Libby likes her, then let things be. Give Libby what you think she needs at home, but also accept that maybe she needs other things as well. It's all part of being a parent."

Alex grunted. Balance. Right.

"And if you'll take a little more advice," Doug said. "I'd try and get along with this Ms. Stein, no matter how much she might remind you of your own ill-spent school days. Teachers have a big impact on kids, but so do guardians. You don't want your attitude rubbing off on Libby."

"As if," Alex said. The scent of baking was already spinning through the air and her mouth was watering. "I'm pretty sure Libby would like to be adopted by Ms. Stein and live in her little army camp of a world forever and ever."

Doug laughed. "Be nice, Alex. Remember, you never know the battles that someone else is fighting. And this Ms. Stein sounds reasonable."

"You're not the one that has to be her parent representative for the rest of the school year," grumbled Alex.

"About that," said Doug. "Just how exactly did that happen?"

"Pour me a glass of wine and I might tell you," Alex said.

CHAPTER TWELVE

Kat clicked the link and was greeted with a long list of apartments. The prices weren't bad at all, not as bad as she'd feared anyway.

"We're not spending another Sunday night sitting around at home," Fran said, collapsing into an armchair. "Come on, let's go out."

"It's a school night," Kat said, scrolling through the listings.

"Last night wasn't a school night."

"But I had lesson planning to do."

Fran rolled her eyes. "Forgive me for this, but you are boring as hell Katarina Stein. What happened to the girl who used to party all night and drink until dawn?"

"You must be thinking of someone else."

"No, that..." Fran paused. "No, actually, you're right. That wasn't you at all. That was this girl Catherine that I knew in college. But we've had some good times. We've gone out drinking and dancing, seen movies, been to exhibitions. Just not for the last... What? Two years? Longer maybe."

Kat put the laptop down on the coffee table. "Fran, I appreciate that you want me to get out and live life to the fullest. But the honest truth of the matter is that I'm really not ready to do that. And even when I am, I need to plan things."

"Planning's boring."

Kat stuck out her tongue. "Necessary though. Tonight's a

school night and not only that, I need to bake cookies for the bake sale tomorrow."

Fran huffed. "Fine. But you owe me one night out."

Kat grinned. "I owe you so much more than that, Fran. And I know that I do. Things will get better."

"You got the job interview, that's a step in the right direction," Fran said. She hesitated and then said: "Do you think you can do it? Walk away from teaching, I mean?"

Kat shrugged. "I honestly don't know." She looked down at the computer screen. "I don't think that I have much of a choice."

"If finances are a problem you know that you can stay here as long as you need to."

"I know, and I love you for it. But I need to get my life back on track. Being a teacher isn't going to pay the bills, I just have to face facts. That car repair bill was enough to throw me for a loop. I love being a teacher, but I need to be able to make a living. My own living."

"You could always go back to teaching later," Fran pointed out.

"Yeah, I guess. It breaks my heart to think…" Kat couldn't finish the sentence.

Fran jumped up and came to sit on the couch next to her, patting her leg and then catching sight of the laptop screen. She leaned in closer.

"Kat? Something you want to tell me?"

Kat closed the computer. "It's nothing, just…"

"Just what? I'm not stupid. Those were apartment listings, even I know that, and I don't speak a word of German."

"I'm just trying to keep my options open is all."

"What kind of options?"

Kat sighed. "If I teach in Germany I might actually be able to pay my own rent."

"But I thought you loved it here?"

"I do."

"But—"

"I'm just keeping my options open," Kat said again.

"Giving up a job you love to stay in a country you love, or keep doing the job you love but go live somewhere you haven't seen for twenty years. Those don't sound like great options."

"Something will work out," Kat said, squeezing Fran's knee. "And besides, I think you're supposed to be comforting me, not the other way around."

"I don't want to think of you leaving. I don't want to be without you," Fran said. "Who's going to answer my calls when I can't sleep? Who's going to come and pick me up after another disastrous date? Who's going to make me cookies?"

"Me," Kat said. She looked back at the laptop and wondered whether or not to say anything. But Fran was so down that she had to. And it might be fun. "Actually, there is something that I was thinking about."

"What?" asked Fran.

Kat cleared her throat. "I, uh, I was thinking that maybe it was time to, um, get back in the game." She thought about the random flushes of heat she'd been having. The admiring glances she'd caught herself giving whenever the right woman walked past. The slow feeling of her sexuality waking back up after a long, long period of hibernation.

"Wait, you mean..." Fran's eyes were round. "Dating again?" she finished with a whisper.

Kat felt herself flush. "Maybe. I mean. I don't know. But I was thinking about maybe giving it a try. Nothing big, no commitments or anything. Just, like, um, an online profile or something?" Her voice was getting squeaky.

"Girlfriend, you've come to the right place," Fran laughed and pulled the laptop toward her.

"It's not enough just to have a profile," Fran said, a half hour later. "You have to look at the other profiles, see what's out there, maybe send a message or two."

Kat took a breath. "No," she said. "I can't, not right now."

It had been harder than she'd thought. Trying to make herself sound attractive, fun, less boring. Trying to forget that she'd never done this before because she'd never had to. Trying to forget that there was a time when she thought she'd never have to date again, because she'd found her Ms. Perfect.

"You okay?" Fran asked.

"Absolutely fine."

She didn't want to talk about it. At the beginning, right after the divorce, she'd only been able to cry. Those days were over now, but only as long as she kept a tight lid on things. As long as she didn't look at their wedding pictures, or her bare finger where a ring should be, or drive past their house or any one of a million other little things.

"You know you need some more hobbies in here. Reading and running don't really cut it."

"What else is there to put?" She was boring, she knew that. Jen had told her as much. She didn't need an online dating profile to remind her that she didn't exactly have much to offer.

"Well, what about a picture at least? Profiles with pictures definitely get more views."

"No way. What if one of my kids saw it?"

"What the hell would a second grader be doing on a dating site?"

"Some of the first kids I taught are over twenty nowadays. And what about my kids' parents, huh? I don't want to take the risk of anyone knowing who I am."

Fran put the laptop down. "Are you sure you actually really want to do this, because I kind of feel like you're not a hundred percent okay with online dating."

"Baby steps," Kat said, getting up. "And who knows, maybe my sense of mystery will attract women from all over the world, dying to know what I look like and what I do with my free time."

Fran snorted. "Right. We'll see how that goes for you then. But seriously, a month from now when you've had no messages at all, can we consider letting me re-write some of that profile and maybe adding a picture or two?"

"We can consider it," Kat said. "Now I've got to get to baking."

"Eugh. Just the smell of your cookies makes me put on ten pounds. I'm going to take a bath."

"Please yourself."

In the kitchen she took out a bowl and began to put ingredients together, mixing by memory, not really thinking about what she was doing.

Was she really ready to date again? She couldn't deny that she was starting to feel a little tingle when she saw an attractive woman, but that didn't mean she had to start flirting yet. On the other hand, why not? She didn't exactly have much to lose.

She pulled a wooden spoon from the jar next to the stove and began mixing her sugar and butter together.

And then there was the job interview. The possibility of moving to Germany. There were so many things. So many options and choices and decisions, and she didn't know how to make any of them. With a wave of loneliness she longed for her old, settled life. The life where everything had already been decided, where all that was left was for her and Jen to grow old together.

She added in the eggs, then the flour, measuring by eye, sure of the recipe she'd baked a thousand times before.

She should concentrate on the here and now. The bake sale was tomorrow. She was dreading it. She'd heard nothing from Olivia's mother. She could only guess at what kind of shit-show Monday would bring. Ms. Blakely didn't look like the organizational type. She wondered if anyone would show up with cookies at all.

Her cheeks flushed with heat, the dough was getting stiff now, harder to mix.

Alex Blakely.

Yoga pants.

Online dating.

Her thoughts were bouncing around like as many ping pong balls as she stared to spoon dough onto baking sheets.

Life had used to be so simple.

CHAPTER THIRTEEN

Mothers and the odd father or two streamed in through the doors, all bearing trays of cookies and cakes and everything in between. Like a policewoman directing traffic, Alex pointed each parent to the appropriate table.

It wasn't exactly rocket science, but she still felt oddly proud of herself. She'd come in early, way before the kids finished school, and had laid out tables in the gym. She'd been prepared with plenty of recyclable plates and forks. The school cafeteria had laid on urns of coffee and hot water for tea, as well as water for the kids. She'd thought of pretty much everything.

For the last half an hour before the bell, she ran around fixing prices to match the price guide she'd come up with and handed out, and making sure that each table had a parent volunteer and enough small change to make it through the sale.

And then she was done. Looking down the room like a general surveying her troops she felt a burst of pride. This was going to be the best bake sale ever.

"It looks amazing."

Alex turned to see the woman who'd sat next to her in the representative's meeting, now cradling a small baby over her shoulder. She grinned. "Thanks."

"No, really. I've got four kids, so I've seen this done plenty. But I don't think I've ever seen it done so smoothly and efficiently."

Alex's grin widened. "Thanks again," she said. Then she

leaned a little lower. "And you know who can suck it? Ms. damn Stein."

The woman blushed and then laughed, the baby stirring on her shoulder. "Your house too, huh?" she said. "I swear to God, if I hear that woman's name again I'll wash my kid's mouth out with soap. Ms. Stein this, Ms. Stein that. It's enough to make me feel like I'm useless. Still... I guess it's good that they like her, right?"

Alex shrugged but didn't get the chance to reply as the bell rang for the end of school and a storm of running footsteps headed her way.

She was rushed off her feet for a few minutes, time enough for what seemed like half the school to descend on the gym. But she did have time to look up as an orderly line came through the door. It was odd, seeing children standing in line and behaving themselves amongst the din of the bake sale. Other kids were running around, faces smeared with chocolate. It was only when she saw Libby frantically waving at her that she realized that, of course, this had to be Ms. Stein's class.

But there was no sign of the woman herself, and Alex was too busy to look for her or even care where she was.

"And there's your change," she said, smiling at the girl and handing her a quarter back.

The girl grinned back in return and was about to run away when Alex stopped her. The frosting ringing her mouth couldn't be allowed to go unchecked.

"Here, sweetie," she said, handing over a napkin. "Make sure you wipe your face with that, okay?"

"'kay," mumbled the child, grabbing the napkin and making off with it.

"Why don't you go get yourself some coffee, you look as though you could use one. I'll take over here."

Alex was about to demur, the last thing she wanted was Ms. Stein finding her deserting her post, but then she saw that the woman doing the talking was Sandy Higgs. She, if no one else, was responsible enough to oversee things for five minutes. So she smiled in thanks and took a step back.

The gym was groaning at the seams with people. There was constant chatter, interspersed with the yells and screams of kids. Alex hoped like hell Ms. Stein was going to be satisfied with all this, it seemed a resounding success to her, but what did she know?

She pulled her phone from her pocket. There was a notification from her dating app, finally. She could use a little fun. But now wasn't the time to deal with that. She clicked open her emails instead, scanning through them quickly. Only one stuck out.

Coming Back Soon? It was from Evie. Obviously. Alex read only the title. She couldn't deal with seeing pictures of places that she couldn't be, not right now. And she definitely couldn't deal with Evie complaining about her not being wherever it was she should be. It wasn't like she had a choice. But Evie just didn't understand. She was going to have to call, to try to explain again, to break things off.

Not that there was a 'thing' to really break off. There wasn't. Neither one of them would be heart-broken, Alex was sure. Still, it was something that needed doing. An ending that she'd been avoiding because ending things completely with Evie would be ending a whole bunch of other things as well. The last nail in the coffin of her free and easy life.

"I have to admit that you've done an incredible job here. You have my thanks."

She was standing, tall and slim, her hair swept up to reveal the graceful curve of her neck, against the sun so that Alex saw only her outline. Her heart beat a little harder and she felt a twinge of something. Fuck me, she thought. Libby was right, Ms. Stein was pretty.

Not that it was important.

"Um, thanks."

"I might have underestimated you," Ms. Stein said.

"Sorry, sorry, Alex, just one thing." A dark-haired woman bustled over. "We've run out of plates, shall I send someone to run to the store?"

Alex shook her head. "Nope. I've got extras. Check the boxes to the right of the basketball hoop at the far end. You should find a whole bunch of new plates there."

The woman sighed with relief and hustled off again.

"Organized," Ms. Stein said. "I like it."

She smiled and Alex thought that perhaps it was the first real smile she'd seen from the woman. It was bright and easy and changed her face into something less sharp and more beautiful. And she'd almost got an apology. She hadn't let Ms. Stein down. A weight lifted off her, one she hadn't known she was carrying.

"Excuse me, Ms. Stein."

A small boy with angelic blonde curls was standing next to his teacher.

"Yes, Jayden?"

"I saved you some of my brownie," he said. "I kept it special just for you."

He held out a handful of brown crumbs wrapped in a napkin and Alex was sure that Ms. Stein with her perfect hair and flawless white shirt was going to tell him to throw it away. But she didn't. She smiled sweetly and thanked the boy for his thoughtfulness, cradling the destroyed chunk of brownie in her hand.

"Um, I'm not sure I'd eat that," Alex said, spotting some unidentified lumps in the crumbs.

"It's the thought that counts," Ms. Stein said with a gentle smile and suddenly Alex could see what the children saw in her.

Maybe she'd underestimated Ms. Stein too. Maybe she'd been too quick to judge. Sure, she was strict, but she obviously adored the kids as much as they adored her. And she hadn't been stinting with her praise, or admitting that she'd been wrong. Not exactly hallmarks of a witch.

"Alex, can I have some more money?" Libby's face was covered in crumbs.

"How many cakes have you eaten already?" Alex asked.

Libby looked down at the pink princess dress she'd chosen to wear especially for the bake sale. "Um, three?"

Alex bit her lip in thought, then nodded. "You can have one more quarter to buy a cookie, but there's no dessert after dinner tonight, deal?"

Libby nodded in joy, accepted the quarter, and ran off.

Ms. Stein cleared her throat.

Alex remembered the look the teacher had given her when Libby had first called her by her Christian name, and was about to explain when Ms. Stein spoke first.

"Ms. Blakely, we really do need to talk about Olivia's school clothes."

"We do?" frowned Alex.

"It's not particularly suitable to send Olivia to school wearing some of the dresses that she has."

Alex felt a prickle of energy on the back of her neck, a sure sign that she was getting mad. "It's not?" she asked. "Because I feel like Libby should wear whatever she pleases. I feel like she should be able to make her own choices. And you don't have a uniform here, unless I'm mistaken?"

"It's not that," Ms. Stein said, her voice patient and calm in a way that made Alex's hand itch to slap her.

"I certainly won't be dissuaded from sending Libby to school in dresses if that's what she chooses to wear."

"Again, that's not the problem," said Ms. Stein. Patronizing, that was the word, Alex thought. "The problem is the kind of dresses. You're sending Olivia to school in designer dresses, clothes that cost hundreds of dollars, and it's really not appropriate."

Shit. Things she should probably have known about. Alex had never owned anything remotely designer, so there was no way she'd have recognized the labels. But of course Claire had dressed her daughter in the best. Obviously. Shit, shit, shit.

"Regardless," Alex barrelled on. She'd chosen her battle, now she had to fight it. "It's Libby's choice."

"I—"

"You have no jurisdiction over what Libby wears as long as

it fulfills your dress code. So that's the end of it. If she wants to wear a damn wedding dress to school, then she will. Is that clear?"

That faint blush of pink was appearing on Ms. Stein's cheeks. Her green eyes were flashing and Alex was suddenly very conscious of the fact that she was standing only inches away and that a heat was emanating from the woman.

"Very clear, Ms. Blakely. I simply—"

"You simply nothing. You deal with teaching, I'll deal with parenting," Alex snapped. "That's the deal, so stick to it."

She marched off before Ms. Stein could stop her. Interfering old witch.

CHAPTER FOURTEEN

Kat sat in the leather chair, spinning slightly as she moved, looking out over downtown through plate-glass windows. Jackson poured her the water that she'd asked for and passed it across.

"It's quite the view, isn't it?" he said.

"Uh-huh. I've seen this building a million times, but never thought that I'd be inside it," Kat said. It felt like the entire building was made of glass, like there was no escaping the light. And everything was so… clean. And it smelled of lemon polish. A far cry from crayon scrawled on walls and the smell of lunch meat from the cafeteria.

"Well, you've got Fran to thank for that," Jackson said. "I've got to be honest here, I'm really not supposed to be interviewing for this job yet. We've got a hiring freeze until January first. But, well, Fran was convincing, and it didn't seem a bad idea to have someone lined up in pole position."

Kat owned precisely one suit and she was wearing it. The waistband of the skirt bit into her skin and the jacket felt tight across the shoulders. If she got this job there was definitely going to be some shopping in order.

If she got this job. She was already thinking about it, already thinking of working in a lemon-smelling office with a suit jacket over her chair.

"I am interested," she said carefully. "But perhaps you could tell me a little more about what the position entails?"

Jackson started talking and she tuned him out. She didn't need to listen, she'd seen the job description, had heard it all from Fran. But she needed a minute to get her mind around things, to see if she could feel comfortable doing this, if she could really give up her classroom for a silent office.

It felt... weird. The last time she'd interviewed for anything it had been teacher's college. And then she'd been in slacks and a sweater and the interviewer had been more interested in her ability to make macaroni necklaces than her being able to explain high level concepts.

She'd walked into her job at Brookfield elementary after completing her internship there. That easy. It had seemed fated at the time.

Had she had ambitions? Sure, at the beginning. She'd thought about being a principal, or working for the state education department. But as soon as she'd stepped into that classroom she'd been sure that she never wanted to leave.

Until now.

Not that she wanted to leave. But it was looking more and more like she had no choice. And to be fair, Jackson was doing his best to make the job sound interesting, challenging, important. Perhaps it was. She just... didn't know if it would be as satisfying somehow.

"And what about a little about you, Katarina? You don't mind me calling you that, do you? We're an informal company here. What about your qualifications and experience?"

It grated on her to hear her first name like that. Working in a school environment meant that most people she knew called her Ms. Stein. It was only those super close to her that used her first name. She shook it off and did her best to answer his question.

Ten minutes later and Jackson was sitting forward in his chair, a sign that things were almost done and Kat could see the dimple on his chin and understood why Fran found the man attractive. But then, Fran found most men attractive.

"I shouldn't really say anything," Jackson was saying. "Due to hiring laws and regulations we are going to have to open the job up to other candidates, of course. But... Well, let's just say that I wouldn't be surprised if you got an offer in the next few weeks. No promises, but you're exactly what we're looking for."

"I am?" Kat asked, surprised.

"You're a qualified teacher with plenty of classroom experience, you definitely look the part, and you have the added feather in your cap of speaking a second language. Yes, I'd say you'd be an excellent fit for the company."

Kat ignored the bit about looking the part. It had seemed unnecessary. But hey, what did she know? She did know that it felt pretty good to be wanted, to be desirable in the professional world. A job where she wore a suit every day, who'd have thought?

Her step was a little lighter as she left the building. Her options were looking slightly more promising at last.

An afternoon off school meant that she had a rare few hours at home in the quiet, something she'd been secretly looking forward to. Kat was still feeling good about herself as she climbed up onto the couch and put a glass of wine on the coffee table.

It was only mid-afternoon, but some rules could be broken occasionally. Something she'd never teach her kids and hoped like hell nobody would catch her doing. But she'd aced a job interview and deserved some kind of reward.

Not that she was necessarily going to get the job, she reminded herself as she pulled her laptop out of her bag along with a stack of papers to grade. And not that she was necessarily going to take it. She was just keeping her options open.

Laptop open she drank a mouthful of chilled wine before checking her emails. There was one address that she didn't recognize.

You've Got a Message! said the title. She frowned at it before something clicked. The stupid dating profile she'd set up with Fran. Her stomach dipped a little with excitement. It was probably nothing, but given her luck today, maybe it was something. She opened the email to find that it simply directed her back to the dating site.

With a sigh, she pulled out her phone and downloaded the dating app itself. Leaving traces of dating sites all over her work laptop probably wasn't smart.

As soon as the app downloaded she got a notification. Her stomach dipped again as she opened it.

LexyLibre>> Hey there mysterious lady... I've always been tempted by the unknown

Kat laughed. Fran was going to owe her a drink. Her profile might have been boring, but hell, one person at least was interested. She drank another mouthful of wine thinking about what to write back. Should she write back? She wanted to. It wasn't a commitment. She had nothing to lose. But her fingers trembled a little, it almost felt like a betrayal.

"Your wife left you," she said aloud. "She cheated on you and left you. You do not have to feel bad about sending a message on a stupid website."

The words seemed to help, to give her a little courage. The wine didn't hurt either. She slurped down another mouthful before typing, then erasing, then typing again.

KittyKat>> Hi. Some mysteries are easier to solve than others. Glad I could tempt you though. I'm not sure how this is supposed to go, this is my first time.

The stupid screen name had been Fran's idea and actually seeing it in print made her blush. The message itself, well, it was at least honest. And maybe a little flirtatious. She hadn't flirted for so long that she was worried she didn't know how to do it anymore.

For a minute or two she stared at her phone before it occurred to her that it was three in the afternoon and most normal people were working. She was unlikely to get an answer soon.

With a sigh, she put the phone away. There was still a warm

glow in her stomach though. Maybe her luck was changing. Maybe things were on the up. Yes, she'd lost her perfect life, but for the first time in what felt like forever she thought that perhaps there could be another life out there for her. One that might be close to perfect. If only she could find it.

The pile of grading by her side was almost complete, but she was stuck on one paper. The children had been asked to write a simple poem, four lines only. The paper she was holding had certainly fulfilled the assignment. What worried Kat more was that the poem itself talked about blood and crashes and rhymed 'bed' with 'dead.' Not signs of a healthy child's mind.

She scratched her nose. It was her job to look out for worrying signs. Some kids, she knew, just had a sense for the morbid. Those she worried about less, it was a stage kids went through sometimes. But this, she checked the name again, this wasn't a morbid child. This was a child that wore pink and yellow princess dresses.

She tapped her fingers on the keys of her laptop, thinking. But there wasn't much choice. This could be nothing, or it could be something, and there was no way to know. As a teacher though, she needed to cover her ass, no matter how much she might want to avoid dealing with this particular parent.

Quickly and briefly she wrote an email to Ms. Blakely requesting an appointment with her after school. Just as it went flying off, her phone beeped. She reached over for it.

LexyLibre>> Your first time? I'll have to be gentle then...
Tell me something about you that nobody knows...
Kat's mouth suddenly felt dry. This... this could be fun.

CHAPTER FIFTEEN

The smell of coffee was hot in the air and Alex quickly slid into her messages as Doug was preparing her a cup.

KittyKat>> I'm an open book. Everyone knows everything about me.

She thought for a second, then typed:

LexyLibre>> Really? What color underwear are you wearing then?!

She was still grinning as she pushed her phone into her pocket.

"You're looking awfully happy for someone that just five minutes ago told me she was thinking about jumping off the pier," Doug said, putting coffee cups down and settling onto a high stool by the counter.

"Eugh. Is there even a pier here?" Alex said. "And I was smiling about something different."

"Dating app," said Doug immediately. Then, seeing the look on Alex's face, added: "The notification tone, it's always the same. Don't think that I haven't done my own share of online dating."

"Well, that's the only excitement in my life currently. And even that's patchy. One response from one woman, and she seems to limit herself to one message a day. It's like getting blood out of a stone."

"And what else is going on, my little chickadee?"

Alex rolled her eyes. "Nothing. And that's kind of the problem. Well, everything and nothing."

"You're going to need to be a little more specific than that."

"I get... antsy, I guess. I don't regret keeping Libby, I would never regret that. But I do regret leaving my old life behind sometimes. A lot of the time." She thought about Evie and her constant messages, the pictures she sent of temples and beaches, designed, Alex was sure, just to tempt her and tease her.

"That sounds pretty normal," said Doug.

"I know, I know. But I need something to take my mind of all of that. I can't sit around for the next ten years doing nothing and waiting for Libby to grow old enough to go to college. That's just going to make me resent her. I need... I don't know, a career, a job, a hobby, something, anything."

"What's the problem with that then?" Doug asked, blowing on his hot coffee.

"I'm not good at anything," Alex said. "No, don't look at me like that. I'm not. I barely scraped through high school, and the only jobs I've ever had were working behind a bar or cleaning in a hostel or something. And I want to be around when Libby needs me, she's too young to be left alone right now, and, eugh, see, I told you. I having some kind of crisis."

"You don't have time for the full therapizing process if you're going to make it to school on time," Doug said with a grin. "So I'll short cut some things here, just to stop you potentially jumping off any piers you might find."

"So there is a pier here, or not?"

"You've had a complete change in your life. It's going to take some getting used to. Part of that process will be trying new things, thinking about things you've never had to think about before. Finding new things to be good at, and in all probability new things that you're terrible at as well."

"Helpful, thank you," Alex said.

"Give yourself a break, Alex. You're already doing a job, you're raising a child. You don't need to feel guilty for not doing something else at the same time. But I'm all for expanding your horizons. We're all good at something. My suggestion for you is that you spend a little time listing the things you enjoy and the things you can do, the skills you have, and seeing where they intersect."

Alex drank some of her coffee, feeling the warmth of it in her throat. "Alright, that is kind of helpful actually. It can't hurt, anyway."

"A resounding compliment to my therapy skills," Doug said with a grimace. Then he caught sight of the microwave clock. "And you'd better go if you're going to make it to school on time."

With a groan, Alex put her coffee cup down. "What does the interfering witch want now?" she said.

"There's only one way to find out," said Doug. "Off with you!"

Ms. Stein slid the poem across the desk to Alex who was already bristling at the idea that there could possibly be anything wrong with Libby at all.

And then she read it.

And her heart sank a little and a lump formed in her throat.

"You can see why I might be a little concerned," Ms. Stein said. She was wearing glasses that framed her eyes and magnified her long lashes.

Alex took a deep breath, trying to control the sadness inside her. She'd been ready to fight, she'd been angry, and now all of a sudden the wind was taken out of her sails.

"It could well be nothing," Ms. Stein said. "Some children just have very, very active imaginations. And most grow out of this stage and learn what is acceptable and what isn't. I'm simply suggesting that—"

"It's not a stage."

It was painfully obvious that Ms. Stein had no idea about Libby's background, nobody had bothered to tell her, or she hadn't read the file, or something. Alex herself had certainly never said anything. As much as she wanted to be angry, she couldn't be. This wasn't the woman's fault, she was doing her job.

"Not a stage? I'm afraid I don't understand."

"Libby's mother died in a car accident about seven months ago."

There was a long silence punctuated by the hum of the floor cleaners out in the corridor and Alex found that her eyes were filling with tears. She dashed them away. She was used to this now, she had accepted it, but every now and again the grief of it jumped out and took her by surprise. A soft, floral scent came closer, and then Ms. Stein was touching her arm, proffering a tissue.

"I'm so sorry," she said.

"Claire was my sister. I'm Libby's aunt, her only living relative as far as we know. Which is why, just so you know, she calls me by my first name." She flashed a glance up at the woman.

"I see."

Alex sniffed and collected herself. "I'm fine now," she said. But she wasn't. She was horrifically embarrassed at having lost her cool. Particularly now, particularly in front of this woman, with her flowery perfume and soft tissues and green and hazel eyes.

"I had no idea," Ms. Stein said, walking her way around to her own side of the desk. "I can see why Olivia's work might from time to time reflect issues that aren't common in other children."

Alex nodded.

It was strange, this sudden calmness. She realized that every other time she'd met the teacher she'd been angry about something. Now though, now she felt like there was a connection, a certain tenderness even.

"However, I'm still professionally required to recommend that you make Olivia an appointment with a psychologist."

And… the moment was gone. Honestly, was the woman ever capable of with-holding judgment? Of maybe being slightly less patronizing? Of being less of a know-it-all? Of maybe, just maybe, coming down off her high horse for two seconds?

"Really?" Alex said, tone ice cold. "Because I was thinking of just, you know, lighting a couple of candles and hanging some crystals over her bed and letting the universe heal her."

"Ms. Blakely, I'm afraid I really can't advise you to do that, it's essential that Olivia—"

Alex rolled her eyes. "I was joking," she said.

"Oh." Ms. Stein's cheeks flushed. "Oh, I, uh... Well, I really don't think this is a joking matter."

"For Christ's sake," Alex said, standing up so fast that her chair almost toppled behind her. "Do you ever get rid of that stick up your ass?"

"Ms. Blakely!"

"No, I'm serious," Alex spat. "Maybe you should take that stick out for a second and realize that you're just as human as the rest of us. Maybe people would like you a little more then. Maybe you'd be a little more interesting, huh? Ever thought of that?"

"Ms. Blakely, this is entirely inappropriate, I must ask you—"

"No," Alex shouted. "*You* must ask *me* nothing. *I* must ask *you* to stop judging my damn parenting skills and to get your damn nose out of my business. Teach my child, that's it. That's your job. So stop interfering with mine."

She strode out of the classroom, slamming the door behind her and not caring that it made her sound like a petulant teenager.

She stopped only when she got to the end of the corridor and turned the corner. Then she leaned against the cold wall and took deep, calming breaths.

Okay, so she wasn't great at this parenting thing. But at least she was trying. That was what no one ever seemed to realize. This was hard. Sometimes so hard that she thought she'd been born broken, that she was missing some kind of mom gene. But she was trying.

She took a last breath. She needed to collect Libby from the after-school program. And then she needed to find a new psychologist. Libby obviously had a few things that she needed to talk about. And Alex would always, always do what was best for her. No matter what anyone else thought.

CHAPTER SIXTEEN

Kat rolled over in bed and pulled her phone to her. Five minutes before the alarm went off. Her heart skipped a little when she saw the notification. The air-con made the room cool, so she snuggled back under the blankets with her phone, opening her messages at the same time.

LexyLibre>> You know, it's terribly difficult to fantasize about someone you've never seen. I just imagine you in a black eyemask. Is it wrong that I find that sexy?!

So, LexyLibre was fantasizing about her, was she? Part of Kat wanted to find that wrong and objectifying, but the other part of her warmed and she felt a throbbing between her legs.

This online dating game was proceeding a lot faster than she'd have thought. But it wasn't bothering her. It was exactly that, a game. There'd been no hint of a meeting, or even of pictures to be exchanged. It was safe, secure, erotic, and exactly what she needed.

KittyKat>> I wouldn't be averse to wearing a mask...

Almost immediately, and unusually, an answer pinged back.

LexyLibre>> Is there something I could wear for you?

So LexyLibre got up as early as she did. Interesting. She thought for a second, her mind running over sexy answers to the question. But the only thing that sprang to mind was yoga pants. And that just wasn't the answer she wanted to put. She didn't even know where the idea had come from, and definitely didn't own any herself.

    KittyKat>> Nothing...

She sent the message before she realized what exactly it implied. She'd meant that she'd come up with nothing, but could see how LexyLibre would read it. The answer pinged back. A winking smiley face. Kat grinned to herself. Oh well, all a part of the game.

"Everything set for this afternoon?" Trisha popped her head around the adjoining door between their classrooms.

"All good," Kat said. She'd stayed at her desk with her lunch sandwich, needing to catch up on some grading. "Just bring yourself after the last bell goes. Oh, and don't forget to put a sign on your classroom door telling your parents we'll be in here."

"On it," Trisha said, disappearing again.

Kat put down her pen. Gazing out of the window she could see the kids playing, could hear the laughs and squeals of delight. It would be a sound she would always treasure, a noise she would miss. It wasn't as if she could go hang out in playgrounds to get her fix of child laughter. That would definitely be creepy if she weren't a teacher.

Weren't a teacher. The very thought of it.

Olivia Blakely ran past the window, dressed in jean shorts and a striped t-shirt, followed by Jayden who was futilely chasing her.

Poor Olivia. She couldn't imagine what it would be like to lose a mother so early in life. Olivia was at the worst age, old enough to understand, old enough to miss someone. Old enough to know when things weren't right.

She'd been making a special effort to keep an eye on Olivia, to ensure that she was happy and that she was handling the change in schools. And in truth, the child seemed like a merry one. She'd made friends easily, and was obviously clever. Now that Ms. Blakely had stopped dressing her in designer clothes, Olivia was no longer teased in the playground. And Kat no longer had a mini-heart attack every time the kid picked up a paintbrush.

Ms. Blakely. Now there was a part of the afternoon she wasn't looking forward to. It would be the first time she'd had to face the woman after their meeting over Olivia's poem. And she knew it shouldn't bother her, knew that the woman had just been angry and throwing around insults, but she couldn't help thinking from time to time about what she'd said.

A stick up her ass.

Ms. Blakely thought she was boring. Too formal, too dull, too... Eugh. Kat put her sandwich down and picked up her phone instead. Just the one message.

LexyLibre>> My masked lady likes to live dangerously, does she? Telling strangers on the internet that she'd like to see them naked... I'm shocked. And quite excited...

Again that twinge of warmth. She really shouldn't be reading these kinds of things in the classroom. She hurriedly put her phone away.

At least someone didn't think she was boring.

Parents streamed in with the usual grumbling and mumbling and the odd shriek as one woman saw another. Kat watched them, thinking how like their children they were, how she could see where each child got his or her unique characteristics from.

"Most of mine are here," Trisha said, putting a pile of hand outs on the corner of the desk. "And the sign's on the door, so those that aren't know where to go. Shall we get this started?"

Kat hesitated and then a figure in yoga pants and a ripped t-shirt slid through the door. She caught a glimpse of dark blue eyes turned her way and her stomach flipped. Christ, she must be really nervous about facing Ms. Blakely again.

"I'll start things off," she said to Trisha, her eyes still on Ms. Blakely who was now coming towards her. An apology perhaps. Well, the woman had been angry, maybe she regretted what she'd said.

"Ms. Stein," Ms. Blakely said coldly. "Just so that you know, I'll be leaving early."

It was on the tip of Kat's tongue to tell Ms. Blakely that she wasn't a student, that she could do as she pleased. But instead, she just said: "Oh."

The woman sniffed and ran a hand through her hair, slicking it back slightly in a way that showed her profile even better. For a second Kat could imagine herself running her own fingers through that hair, could almost feel it...

"I need to pick Libby up."

"Uh-huh," Kat said, on guard, cautious.

"From, uh, from her psychologist appointment."

Kat sighed in relief. So the woman had done it, she was doing what was right. She felt a wave of appreciation and a calmness knowing that Olivia would have professional help if she needed it. She was going to thank Ms. Blakely, but the woman was already walking away, finding herself a seat in the crowd of second and third grade parents.

Kat clapped her hands and an unsteady silence descended. Time to get this started. At the back of her mind was the thought that this might be the last time she did this. But she pushed the thought away, now was no time for sentimentality.

"Good evening, for those of you that don't know me, I'm Ms. Stein, the second grade teacher here at Brookfield. As some of you may know, originally I am from Germany. And in my country it is traditional that all elementary school children spend a week each year out in nature. We call this School in Nature, and it is a tradition that I'm happy to have continued at Brookfield."

There was a stirring at this. Most parents already knew about the trip and she could see that some of them were relieved at the thought of having a few days break from child care and parenting. She couldn't exactly blame them.

"We won't be gone for the whole week," she said. "But the second and third grade classes will be spending three nights in the Tallaheenee forest at a special nature center designed for children. Now, Ms. Benson has handouts with answers to the most common questions, including a packing list, drop off and pick up times, and important phone numbers, so if you could pass these around."

She handed off the papers and let the parents help themselves, listening to their chatter, glad that they were excited about the opportunity. One hand was raised. She saw it and nodded at the woman in the second row.

"Is this required?" the woman asked.

There was always one. Kat sighed. "It's not a requirement," she said. "Although we strongly encourage all children to go. It's important that kids learn to understand and appreciate nature and the environment, it's important that they get fresh air. But it's also an important part of their development that they spend a little time away from home with their peers. This is a bonding experience."

The woman still looked unsure.

"The handout you have goes into detail about financial help should it be required," Kat went on. "And of course, this is a safe environment. Both Ms. Benson and I will be along for the trip, along with a handful of parent volunteers. Which is what we should get to next. I'll pass along a sign up sheet, if you're prepared to join us please put your name, phone number and email on the sheet."

The next twenty minutes or so were full of random questions and allaying the fears of the nervous parents. Trisha took the lead and Kat retrieved the sign up sheet, glancing down at it just as she heard the door creak. Looking over, she could see Ms. Blakely edging out of the classroom.

Olivia's psychologist appointment, of course. Except... Kat looked down the sign up sheet and then shook her head.

Quietly, she slipped out of the room, seeing Ms. Blakely just rounding the corner of the corridor. With an irritated sigh, she chased after her.

"Ms. Blakely!"

She caught up just by the main entrance, waving the sign up

sheet as she got there.

"What? I told you I had to leave early."

Kat bit her tongue. She was not going to be goaded into an argument with the woman. Instead, she said calmly: "You didn't sign up."

"So?" Ms. Blakely was already edging away again.

"So, you're the parent rep, you have to go. It's on the list of responsibilities I gave to you."

Those deep blue eyes stared long and hard and Kat was sure she was going to say no or maybe even hit her. There was a strange crackling of energy between them, something that almost scared her.

"Fine," Ms. Blakely said, turning and walking away. "You have my contact information."

And Kat let out a breath she hadn't known she was holding.

CHAPTER SEVENTEEN

"Alex!"

Alex pulled the comforter over her head.

"A-lex!"

She groaned. She hadn't gone to bed until three and she'd known that she'd regret it but the regret was a whole lot more tangible right now.

"Alex!"

A small missile landed on her bed and then yanked the covers off her head. Libby peered down at her, eyes starting to fill with tears.

"What is it, kiddo?" Alex said, struggling to sit up.

"We're going to miss School in Nature," Libby started to sob. "It's too late and we're not going to be there in time and…"

Alex looked at the clock. Shit. She had a faint memory of the alarm going off and stretching out an arm to make the beeping stop. She took a breath, worked things out in her head, and had a plan immediately.

"We're not missing anything," she said. "Go get dressed while I hop in the shower, and we're going to be out of the house in ten minutes. No more." Thank God she'd taken care of all the packing the night before.

"What about breakfast?"

"We'll eat on the run," Alex said. "Now go. Hop to it!"

Eleven minutes later they were in the car and Alex was screeching out of the driveway and trying to eat a breakfast bar all at the same time. Libby was still sniffling in the back.

"Have a little iPad time," Alex said, passing the gadget back. "Calm down. We're going to get there, don't worry."

Libby plugged in her headphones and settled back and Alex drove as fast as she legally could, praying to hit every damn green light. And cursing herself for not getting to bed earlier, for letting Libby down.

It hadn't entirely been her fault. The call to Evie had gone on longer than she'd expected. There had been recriminations and tears and Alex had realized only half way through the conversation that Evie's feelings for her had been much deeper than she expected.

She'd apologized until she was blue in the face. She'd told Evie the truth, that there was nothing she could do, nowhere she could go. She'd even offered Evie a place to stay if she wanted to come back to the States. And that had finally ended things. Evie had realized that she didn't want to be with Alex enough that she was willing to settle down.

But it had taken hours to get to that point. Exhausting, draining hours that had left Alex wanting to scream. She'd tried to be reasonable, logical, but all the while knowing that these weren't her choices, that if she were left to her own devices she'd be on a plane and back to Evie in a snap. Not because of Evie, of course, who she'd honestly thought was no more than a little fun. But to her real life. Her old life.

She was interrupted by a shriek from Libby in the backseat. She checked the mirror just in time to see Libby pointing at a school bus pulling out of the school gates. Shit. They'd missed it. Alex gritted her teeth and pressed the accelerator.

Libby wasn't going to miss this trip. She'd been looking forward to it for weeks. And if Alex had to follow the bus all the way to wherever the hell they were supposed to end up, then she would.

"We're not stopping until we get there," she told Libby. "Don't worry. We won't lose them. Just keep an eye on that bus."

Alex had to admit that things were better than she'd thought. There were no tents, for a start. The adults had tiny single rooms, and the kids were in a long dormitory with bunk beds. The center was organized. She had her own little group of four kids that she was responsible for, but that basically meant making sure all of them made it to the next activity center. The staff were professional and knew what they were doing.

Okay, so she hadn't wanted to come. But it had been the right thing to do and she hadn't been able to think of a reason not to. Ms. Stein had caught her off guard. So here she was surrounded by small children in the middle of a forest. Perfect.

She glanced around, seeing a blonde head bobbing on the far side of the activity circle. Ms. Stein. Looking as put-together as always in jeans that Alex was fairly sure had been ironed, and a flannel shirt rolled up to her elbows. As long as she stayed on the far side of the circle, that was fine. Keeping out of Ms. Stein's way was Alex's sole intention during the next three and a half days.

"Hey, look!"

A tow-headed young boy who Alex vaguely remembered was called Robbie was showing her a picture. It was a fox. Or possibly a deer. Or very maybe it was some kind of bird.

"Awesome," she said with enthusiasm. "But make sure you're paying attention to the group leader."

Things could definitely be worse. She pulled her phone out of her pocket. There might even be a little time for some fun.

KittyKat had started out as nothing. The woman had a near-empty profile and Alex had almost ignored it. Now she was glad that she hadn't. Whoever the mysterious woman was, she was...

exciting. Both naïve and up-front in ways Alex found more than interesting. In fact, KittyKat's messages were becoming the high point of her day.

Not that she had so much else to do with her day. She hadn't worked on the list Doug had told her to make. She hadn't worked on anything. By the time she'd grocery shopped, been to the gym, dealt with Libby's needs and maybe emailed an old friend or two, time just seemed to have slipped away.

But she was going to come up with a plan. She wasn't going to just be a housewife. Not that there was anything wrong with that. It just wasn't for her. She needed… something. A project, an idea.

"Miss! Miss! Look at this! Miss Olivia's mom!"

Another girl, Alison, she thought, was waving a picture in her face.

"It's beautiful," Alex said.

The girl grinned back. Alex let out a breath. God only knew how Ms. Stein had the energy for this constant… energy. She had enough with one child to care for.

Her phone was still in her hand, the kids were safely diverted, she glanced at the screen. A little heavy flirting with KittyKat would help pass the next three and a bit days, she decided. Maybe even more than flirting, maybe it was time to ask to meet, or at least for a picture.

Her phone buzzed. She looked at the notification bar. No signal.

She'd have been angry if she had had time. But just as she noticed that there was no service in the forest there was a high-pitched scream and then a flush of activity as children ran from their stations toward the noise. Alex followed, instinct driving her toward the growing crowd.

She pushed her way through, seeing Ms. Stein sitting on the ground, her face pale, clutching at her wrist. In a millisecond she took in what had happened.

"Ms. Benson, can you address the children, tell them all is fine and get them back to their activities," she said sharply. The teacher nodded and Alex turned to the staff member who had been running Ms. Stein's group activity. "Do you have a first aid station?"

The staff member nodded. "We do, but it's basic at best."

Alex was already on her knees, pulling Ms. Stein's hand away from her injury and looking at what was underneath. She sucked breath in between her teeth. She was no doctor, but the wrist was already swelling. Basic first aid wasn't going to cover this.

"Closest hospital?" she demanded.

"No," Ms. Stein said. Her voice was a little shaky. "That won't be necessary."

"Just down the road you came up, you'll see it posted," the staff member said. "It's about a twenty minute drive."

"No, no, I'm fine."

Alex looked down at the woman, whose face was getting even paler as she tried to stand up. "You're not fine. You need an x-ray at the least. Make a fuss and you'll scare the children."

She jogged over to Ms. Benson and explained the situation.

"Shall I call for an ambulance, Alex?" the woman asked.

Alex grinned, liking the woman. At least she got called by her first name. "My car's here, remember?" she said, glad now that she'd been running so late. "It'll be faster, not to mention cheaper, for me to drive her down and back again when she's done. In the meantime, will the rest of you be okay with the kids?"

"We'll hold down the fort. I'll redistribute the groups for the rest of the activities, and it's getting close to dinner time anyway. We'll be just fine."

By the time Alex got back, Ms. Stein was sitting on a fallen log, her color a little better, but wincing in pain as she tried to move her arm. Alex took a deep breath. She kind of wished someone else could do this. She didn't relish the idea of spending the next however many hours in the company of Ms. Stein. But there was nothing else to be done. She had a car. She wasn't about to send the woman to hospital on a school bus.

She jingled her car keys and Ms. Stein looked up at her. For a second Alex saw how delicate her skin was, how there was faint down on her cheeks, how the green in her eyes dimmed just a little with pain. Then she sighed. What a fucking day. She could really do with less excitement in her life.

"Come on then," she said roughly. "Let's go."

CHAPTER EIGHTEEN

Kat wasn't sure what was worse. The jolt of pain that went through her arm every time she moved, or the spike of pain that went through her back every time she tried to get comfortable on the stupid plastic chair in the waiting room.

It had been an accident, she'd tripped, nothing more than that. And now here she was, missing the first night of what was probably her last School in Nature, because she was sitting at the hospital with the one person in the world she'd never want to spend an evening with.

"Here."

Alex threw a vending machine candy bar at her. Kat closed her eyes for a second. Ms. Blakely, Alex as she'd insisted on now being called though Kat hadn't actually said it aloud yet, was being nice. She was doing the right thing. She was helping. It was unfair to be angry with her or distant from her or anything other than polite. Even if she did wish the woman was an ocean and at least a thousand miles away.

"Thanks." She opened the chocolate bar with one hand and her teeth.

"So, um, is there anyone I should be calling?" Alex said, crossing her legs.

She was in grey yoga pants today, with a black t-shirt that was less torn than usual. It was also shorter than usual. Short enough that Kat had glimpsed the blue and green of a tattoo earlier in the afternoon when Alex had bent to retrieve something.

"Sorry, what?"

"Someone I can call for you," Alex said again. "I don't know, husband, mom, whatever."

"I'm divorced." That word still tasted strange.

"Ah."

"You can go," Kat said. "I mean, you don't need to wait around. You can go back to the kids. I can call when I'm done."

"No cell reception up there."

"Or get a cab or something," said Kat.

Alex just shrugged and concentrated on her own chocolate bar and Kat saw even white teeth biting into dark chocolate. She sighed and then collected herself.

"Thank you," she said. "Thanks for doing this. It was kind of you to drive me and kinder of you to wait with me."

"No probs," Alex said, looking around the half-full waiting room. She turned back to Kat and grinned. "Hey, while you're here, maybe we could get that stick removed from your ass?"

She said it in a teasing way, not mean, and Kat rolled her eyes and felt a sizzling of irritation but let it go.

"Sorry, bad joke," Alex said, settling back into her seat. "I hate hospitals. They make me feel jumpy."

"I know what you think of me."

Kat blinked at the sound of her own voice. She hadn't really meant to say that out loud. But now that she had, perhaps it was right. Perhaps this little... thing needed some clearing up. Perhaps she was just tired and in pain.

"You do?" Alex said.

"Yes, you think I'm a boring old fuss-pot that's too strict and old fashioned," Kat said. "You as much as told me that."

Alex looked at her from the side of her eye. "Yeah? I guess you're right, I kind of did. I was angry at the time though." She sniffed. "The kids like you though," she added. "And... And I guess you could have a point about discipline. Libby's much more organized than she used to be."

"Kids need limits, that's what makes them feel safe."

Another shrug and another sideways glance. "I know what you think of me," Alex said. "I'm some crazy new-age weird-o without the first clue about parenting."

"No," Kat said. Then she caught Alex looking at her and half-smiled. "Well, maybe a little. At first."

"You're right," Alex said, stretching out her legs. "I don't have the first clue."

"Nobody does. It's not like there's a handbook for raising a child. It's all just trial and error. You're not alone. And frankly, you're not doing a bad job. Libby is obviously a happy child, she's smart, she's got good hygiene."

Alex snorted. "Good hygiene, really? That's the best you can do for a compliment."

It was Kat's turn to shrug, a movement that made her wrist burn.

"Thanks though," Alex said, pulling out her phone.

The conversation was obviously over. But it had been a start maybe. A beginning of an understanding. Kat pulled out her own phone. They could be waiting hours yet and she might as well take advantage of actually having reception down here.

She clicked into her message box.

> *LexyLibre>> What does a girl need to do for a little attention around here? I'm getting kind of lonesome by myself. Leave me long enough and I'll have no choice but to take matters into... my own hands.*

Kat's breath caught in her throat and a flood of wetness bubbled between her legs. She could feel herself flushing. Her eyes darted from side to side, but no one was paying attention to her. Why would they? Alex's face was buried in her own phone. Kat bit her lip, then started to type.

> *KittyKat>> I don't mind you taking matters into your own hands. Sometimes the best way to learn is to watch...*

It was daring, unlike her, but she couldn't help herself. In the background she heard a familiar notification sound, she opened her message box again, but LexyLibre hadn't answered yet. As she watched though, a message came in and the notification sounded again, louder this time.

LexyLibre>> Watch and learn, mysterious one. And then perhaps there are a few things that I can teach you...

Kat's heart rate sped up. Fingers quick now and feeling more and more daring, she typed another message.

KittyKat>> I doubt it. I'm a teacher myself. And a very good one.

As soon as the message sent there was the notification tone again and she went back to her message box confused at the noise. Then there was a gasp and she looked up to see Alex staring at her, mouth open and face aghast.

"It's you."

"What?" Kat asked, looking around in case the nurse had called her name and it was her turn.

"It's you," Alex said again. "You're KittyKat."

Blood rushed to Kat's cheeks, her mouth went dry. "How the hell do you know that?" she asked, not even thinking to deny it. How could she know? Had she been eavesdropping, reading messages over her shoulder? How?

"You fucking idiot," Alex said. "Have you not been listening?"

"Don't call me that, and listening to what exactly?"

"The notification tones bouncing back and forth between our phones as we both sit here messaging each other like the fucking idiots that we are."

It was Kat's turn to gasp, an inhale of breath that did little to calm her or fill her lungs. "You mean…"

"Yes. I'm LexyLibre."

There was a long moment of complete silence that was broken by the sound of a sliding door and the rattle of a clipboard and then a voice calling out.

"Katarina Stein? Katarina Stein?"

Kat had no choice but to follow the nurse into the exam room, head spinning and stomach churning at the thought of what had just happened.

"We just forget it ever happened," Alex said.

Lights flashed past them on the road and Kat cradled her arm. Not broken. A bad sprain. Enough to be strapped up, a couple of painkillers, and she was feeling a little better. Physically at least.

"All of it?" she asked.

It wasn't a bad idea. She was embarrassed, she felt humiliated, and she wanted to throw herself in front of traffic. But maybe, maybe if they both agreed that they would just pretend nothing happened then she could live with herself. Then she could face Ms. Blakely again at parent-teacher night. Her stomach flipped at the thought.

"All of it," Alex said.

"Fine. Deal."

They completed the rest of the drive in silence. Kat couldn't believe her luck. Out of all the women in the world, the one that she'd opened up to, the one she'd been daring and so unlike herself with, was the one woman that she wished would drop off the face of the earth. How was that even fair?

She was angry, with herself, with the world, with Alex. And, she had to admit, a little disappointed. The messaging, the thrill of flirting, had been a high point for her, a sign that things were changing, that things were looking better. So much for that.

Alex pulled the car up in front of the camp building. The lights were out, the kids long asleep. Kat struggled with her seatbelt. Alex opened her door, walked around, and bent over, unclasping the seatbelt for her.

Kat felt flustered, standing up too quickly, grabbing onto the door for support, forgetting that Alex would still be so close. And when she looked up there she was. A pale face in the moonlight only an inch from hers. Lips parted softly, eyes framed by long dark lashes.

And that crackling energy was there again and she was scared again but there was more to it than that, she suddenly realized.

This was LexyLibre. The only woman that had ever thought

Kat was exciting. Mysterious. Not boring. And she couldn't help herself. She wasn't ready to let go of that yet, wasn't ready to surrender to being her dull self again.

So she did the most exciting thing she could think of.

She leaned forward and kissed her.

CHAPTER NINETEEN

That kiss. It went on for what felt like hours under the moonlight. The softness of Ms. Stein's lips brushing against her own, then the pressure beginning as they both let the kiss overtake them. Alex pressed her body against the other woman's, feeling how each curve fit together, sensing that slight rocking forward as Ms. Stein pressed her hips toward her, wanting more.

Her hands slid to the narrow waist, thumbs stroking hipbones achingly slowly and Ms. Stein cupped her face and brought her closer and it was the closest to heaven that Alex had ever been. There was no thought, no emotion, no nothing, just the physical sensation of the kiss, of a woman's body against her own, and a gradual awakening, and an opening up of the possibility of this really happening.

Until, with a soft, beautiful sigh, they pulled apart.

Alex could feel herself smirking. "Thank you, Ms. Stein." She couldn't help herself.

"Katarina. Kat."

Alex nodded, and Kat slid away from her grasp, closing the car door and then walking away on legs that looked shaky. The moonlight glanced off her hair and Alex watched her go, the slow sway of her hips, the soft silhouette of her body.

So that, that was what it had all been about. The crackling, the energy, the irritation. It had all been for that. For the flower-smelling softness of that kiss that had hinted at the need, the desperation behind it.

Alex was still leaning against the car. She didn't trust herself to move. Her legs were trembling and her core was hot and liquid, and her breathing was ragged. It was a long time before she followed the teacher back into the youth center.

Come morning, the world was different. Ms. Stein was the center of attention with students running back and forth to get her juice or cereal for breakfast, anxious to help. For the rest of the day, for the next two days, she was Ms. Stein. And Alex let it happen. Every now and again she caught a look, a glance, a wink that was all Kat.

She wanted to chase her, but something stopped her. It all seemed wrong, here and now. So she sat back and waited. She wasn't generally the most patient of people, but she thought she could do this, thought she could wait for the slim, blonde teacher.

But by the time children were throwing their bags back onto the school bus, nothing had been said and nothing had been done. And Alex thought maybe she'd misjudged things. Maybe Ms. Stein regretted what had happened.

"Alex, can I go on the bus?"

Libby's pigtails were crooked and there was an unidentifiable stain on her t-shirt and she was grinning the biggest grin that Alex had seen for months.

"I've got the car here, kiddo."

"I know, but please, Alex? I wanna go on the bus."

Alex sighed. "Okay, check it out with Ms. Stein and if she says it's okay, then I say it's okay. I'll pick you up at school."

Libby ran off happy and joyful and Alex saw her talk to the teacher and climb up on the bus, so she got into her car and started the engine. There was nothing to wait for now. No point in sticking around.

But she took a long look in the rear-view mirror just in case.

Ms. Stein was directing the children onto the bus. She didn't even turn. With a sigh, Alex pulled away from the parking lot and started her way home.

A day passed, then two, then three, then it was the weekend and Libby was complaining to go swimming so Alex took her to the shore. And still nothing. No emails, no calls, no instant messages from KittyKat. Not a thing.

She must really regret that kiss, Alex thought as she lay on her bed. She felt... hurt somehow, disappointed. It stung more than it should even though Kat had been nothing but a judgemental irritation, even though there was no reason at all to like her. Even though...

Alex sighed and threw her pen down. She was surrounded by papers. Doug had said she needed to make lists, things she enjoyed, things she was good at, skills she had. She was doing her best. But so far her skills list consisted of mixing a mean margarita and microwaving dinosaur chicken nuggets.

She had to face facts, there was nothing she was qualified to do, nothing she had much experience doing. If she wanted to work then she might as well go back to bar-tending or waitressing, both of which would be close to impossible with a small child in the house.

Maybe, just maybe she should have lived her life differently. But if she closed her eyes and thought about the beach sunsets, the parties, the friends and experiences and everything else, she couldn't bring herself to regret any of it.

But when she thought about all that, another image popped up. The beach, the sunset, and... Kat. The touch of her lips, the pressing of her body against Alex's own, the tickle of her tongue, the rocking of her hips. Alex's breath came a little faster.

Slowly, she slid her hand down her body, feeling the smooth skin of her stomach, the crinkled waistband of her pajama pants, creeping underneath that waistband, finding warmth and the roughness of hair before... liquid wetness, slick beneath her fingers.

She sighed with contented pleasure, letting her fingers dance their familiar dance, her hips bucking upward as she imagined Kat moving against her. Her stomach tensed, her thigh muscles twitched, her hand moved faster. Kat naked in the moonlight, her body slipping into the sea. Kat twisted in a sheet in peaceful sleep. Kat astride her, head thrown back and bucking against her.

Alex's breath caught and then the world exploded around her, ringing in her ears.

After, hand still inside her pajamas, sweaty and breathless and only half-fulfilled, she came to a decision. Enough was enough.

"Ms. Blakely, did we have an appointment?"

Ms. Stein, Kat, was wiping down the whiteboard. She was wearing the same pencil skirt that Alex had first seen her in and Alex longed to grasp that waist, to pull the woman toward her, to... She swallowed.

"No, no appointment," she said.

"Is there a problem with Olivia?"

The name still grated and Alex had to breathe away a flash of irritation. "No."

Finally, Kat turned around. Her shirt was open just enough that Alex could glimpse her collarbone. "Then what can I help you with?"

As if nothing had happened, as if that night was a fantasy, a dream. Except Alex could still see the edge of a bandage around the teacher's bad wrist. She found that she was nervous, that there were butterflies flitting around her stomach. Which was stupid because she'd asked plenty of women out. This was different, though she didn't know why.

"I, uh, I think we should go out."

It came out stumbling and stuttering and not at all as elegant as she'd wanted it to sound. Kat raised an eyebrow and Alex prepared herself for the arguments. It was a bad idea. Kat was Libby's teacher. They had a professional relationship. They were close to hating each other. She had no counter-arguments to any of these. No argument at all except she couldn't stop thinking about that damn kiss.

"Go out?" Kat said.

Alex licked her lips and nodded. "I, um, I..." Screw this. She looked around and saw nobody, then slammed the classroom door shut and glared at Ms. Stein. "You kissed me." It came out as an accusation.

"I did, didn't I." It wasn't a question. Kat seemed surprised even at herself.

"You kissed me and then ignored me." It stung even more now that she put it into words.

And now Kat wasn't looking at her, she was looking at the ground and her cheeks were flushed and Alex kind of wanted to slap her, but also really wanted to throw her down on the desk and do unspeakable things with her.

"I shouldn't have done that," Kat said quietly.

"Kissed me?" Alex said, anger boiling up now.

"No," said Kat. "Ignored you." She looked up and she was half-smiling. "I'm sorry. I just... I'm not used to this. To any of it. I..."

Alex rolled her eyes. "Fine," she said. "Why don't you explain yourself over dinner? Friday at seven?"

There was a brief pause and Alex could hear kids playing out on the playground. Her heart had stopped beating.

"Okay."

With a rush of blood her heart beat again and Alex felt like she'd just finished a marathon.

CHAPTER TWENTY

Kat's Uber pulled up in front of what looked like a ramshackle wooden barn with a neon bar sign in the window. She looked down at the address Ms. Blakely had sent her. No. Alex. The address Alex had sent her.

"Are you sure this is the right place?" she asked the driver.

"Absolutely," the woman said. She glanced back in the rearview mirror. "Date?"

Kat nodded.

"If you want, I'll wait around for five minutes. That way you'll have a ride out of here if you need it."

"Seriously?"

"From one woman to another, yeah, of course. This place looks kind of dodgy, I wouldn't want to be walking in there either."

Kat pulled enough money to cover the bill plus a healthy tip out of her wallet. "Thank you so much. If I'm not out in five, you can go, please don't wait too long."

The driver grinned and Kat got out of the car.

This was all so not her. The date, the place, the fact that she'd agreed to go with Alex in the first place. Yet she was the one that had started that kiss. A kiss that she badly wanted to regret and just couldn't. Alex was infuriating, irritating, and nothing like anyone she'd ever been interested in before. But she couldn't let her go. Couldn't let the feeling of that kiss go.

Maybe it was just because LexyLibre had found her interesting, maybe it was just the attention.

She pushed open the door and found that the inside of the place was nicer than she'd expected. Rock music was playing, but not too loud, and there was a central bar with a bunch of tables around it and booths against one wall.

Her eyes were drawn immediately to Alex. She was in a booth. Tight black pants encased her legs. A long t-shirt hung off one shoulder. Her hair was half slicked back, her eyes ringed in kohl. Kat's brain took one look and decided to take the night off. Other, more important, parts of her anatomy primed themselves with anticipation. Her legs started to tremble again.

Somehow she managed to get to the booth, and she collapsed gratefully into a seat.

"I'm guessing this isn't your normal kind of place," Alex said in greeting.

Kat shook her head, not trusting herself to speak as she took in Alex's cheekbones, her lashes, every detail about her making her want to grab the woman and take her right now on the table. Jesus, this woman had an effect on her.

"The food's pretty good, I hear. At least that's what my neighbor Doug said. The music rocks, and it seemed a good idea to go somewhere casual. I hope you don't mind."

Be interesting, Kat told herself. Be daring. Be... not boring. "It's fine," she said. "Nice. You, um, you look nice. Good." Her mouth was drying up.

Alex pulled over a pitcher of beer and poured some into an empty glass. "There. Alcohol will help. Not too much. But relaxing is a good thing."

Kat took the glass and drank. "This is weird," she said, deciding that honesty was the best policy. "Going on a date with the parent of a student."

Alex laughed and the tension burst like a bubble. "Sure it's not weird because you and I have yet to have a conversation without one of us insulting the other in some way?"

"Well, there is a small 'walking on eggshells' element involved," Kat admitted.

Alex shuffled forward in her seat. "Alright, cards on the table moment. We got off to a bad start, I get that. We're obviously quite different people. But, hey, opposites attract, right? And... well, to be completely honest with you, I can't get that kiss off my mind. I know the whole internet dating thing was kind of odd, but we seemed to get along just fine in writing. So I figured maybe we should give things another try."

Kat bit her lip and Alex reached to take her hand, gently twining fingers in with hers.

"I like you, Ms. Stein, that's what I'm trying to say. I find you attractive. I would like to see where this takes us. That's all."

Kat's heart beat a little harder, then she nodded. "I appreciate your honesty. And I'll return it. I have no idea why I did what I did. No idea why I kissed you like that. No idea why we seem to irritate each other so much. But I do know that... I can't regret that kiss. I may also like you. Maybe."

"May also? Maybe?" Alex snorted a laugh. "Well, it's a start, I suppose."

Alex took her hand as they walked out of the bar. The night was cool and stars were pricking through the sky. Almost wintertime, Kat thought.

"I should call an Uber."

"Wait," said Alex. "There's something I need to do first."

She stepped in and they were almost nose to nose and even in the darkness, Kat could see Alex's deep blue eyes glinting. Her body longed for what was going to happen, but her mind was somewhere else.

They'd connected, really connected, she'd be the first to admit that she'd had a wonderful evening. Alex was funny, charming, and her travel stories were fascinating. But here was someone who bungee jumped, who went white-water rafting, who had scaled pyramids and slept on beaches and got lost in the jungles of Malaysia. How could someone like that possibly find her interesting?

"I've had a wonderful time," she said, delaying the moment. "You've lived a very interesting life."

"Yeah," Alex said. She sighed. "Sometimes I feel like this, right now, isn't really my life at all."

"I can see why." Giving up a lifestyle to take care of a child was a big decision. One that Kat respected Alex for.

"I wish I was like you."

Kat frowned. "What?"

"I wish I was like you, sometimes," Alex said. "I wish I knew what I wanted, I wish I had a calling, I wish there was something that I was as good at as you are at teaching."

It was Kat's turn to move now. She carefully scooped a lock of hair behind Alex's ear, her fingertip barely touching her skin, a tremor running up her arm.

Alex reached up to cup her cheek, and then their lips were meeting again and Kat could feel herself disappearing into the sensation of being kissed.

It had been so long since she'd been with anyone but her wife. She'd been worried that she wouldn't remember how to do anything, that everything would be unfamiliar again. The first kiss could have been instinct, but this second one showed her that there was nothing she'd forgotten.

Alex's hands went lower, skirting her waist, pulling her in and Kat's body responded, a heat growing between her legs that was impossible to ignore. She put her hands into Alex's hair, pulling her even closer, tasting her, smelling her, filling all her senses with the woman.

She felt a pressure and then Alex's leg was sliding between hers and she let it happen. For one glorious moment, she allowed her legs to be parted. And then she came to her senses.

"We're making out in a parking lot like desperate teenagers," she whispered, pulling away from Alex's lips.

"I feel like a desperate teenager," Alex said with a groan, but she backed off, stepped away. "Come home with me."

How she wanted to. But no. She was afraid, she could admit

that. Afraid of herself and what she might do and what all this might mean. But she also wasn't ready, not yet. No matter how much her body wanted Alex she just wasn't ready to jump into bed with another woman.

"Olivia will be home," she said.

"She'll be asleep, the babysitter will have made sure of it."

Okay. No excuses. Kat swallowed. Honesty was best. "I want to. But I'm not ready."

Alex knew about the divorce, she knew everything, and she nodded. "I'll wait," was all she said.

Fran was still out when Kat got home and she wasn't unhappy to have the house to herself for a little while. Her body still sang with wanting Alex. She was planning to take a shower, to put herself to bed, to turn out the lights, and then to remember that kiss and see where her feelings took her.

This, this could be something. As strange and odd and weird as it was, there was something about Alex that she wanted. It frightened her.

She opened up her laptop and checked her email while the shower was warming up. A handful of new messages, nothing important. Except one.

She read it twice and then closed her computer.

She didn't know how to feel.

In the shower, warm water cascaded down her skin and her head was buzzing. She should be happy, she should be ecstatic. But it was hard to find the energy.

She'd got the job. She'd officially been offered the role of corporate trainer from February fifteenth. Right when first semester ended. The day after Valentine's.

She stood in the shower until her fingers wrinkled and the water turned cold.

CHAPTER TWENTY ONE

Alex sighed as her phone rang again. Unknown number. She was literally on her way out of the house and she really didn't have time for a phone call. Particularly one that was likely to be telemarketing or otherwise junk. She thrust her phone into her pocket.

"I won't be long," she called out.

"It's fine, take your time," Doug shouted back. "Libby and I need to catch up, plus I haven't seen Frozen 2 yet, so..."

Alex laughed. "You're in for a treat then," she said as she opened the front door.

Libby had been obsessed with Frozen just like every other kid on the block, and Alex had seen the second movie at least a dozen times. It'd be good for Libby to have someone else to show it to. And she was damn glad that she'd signed up for that streaming membership. What the hell did parents do before Netflix and Amazon and everything else?

She slowly backed the car out of the drive. She'd been honest, she wasn't going to be long. She'd been able to persuade Kat to have a coffee, but not much else. Busy, had been the reply, and it was a school night, she guessed. Still, she hoped it wasn't a brush off.

Things had been going oddly well, given that their first three meetings had involved her yelling at the teacher. Kat was... different. There was a little naivety about her, a simplicity that was honest and touching. Okay, she wasn't Alex's normal type, but did that really matter?

She was slowly coming to the realization that Kat might be more than a fling. Not that they'd even had a fling yet, since Kat steadfastly refused to go any further than a goodnight kiss. Maybe that was another brush off.

The problem was, she just didn't know. She guessed that as much as Kat wasn't her usual type, she herself was far from Kat's usual type. At the lowest moments, when she was cleaning the bathroom at two in the morning because she couldn't sleep, she wondered how Kat could possibly be interested in her at all.

She had no prospects, no drive, no ambition. She had zero clue about what she was doing with Libby, though Lord knows she was trying. Someone as put together, as efficient and focussed as Kat couldn't be interested in her, surely?

At other times, like right now as she took a turn towards the main street, she felt a hot fire burning in her stomach as she thought about seeing the woman. Keeping her distance was the problem. The more she saw Kat, the more she longed to touch her skin, to taste her, to have her. Enough so that sometimes she was shaking by the end of dinner or coffee or even, once, a parent-teacher meeting.

She pulled into the parking lot of the coffee shop. No sign yet of Kat's banger, so she pulled out her phone. No more missed calls. There was a text though. Thinking it might be Kat, she opened it up.

Still friends? A picture was attached. Evie sitting on top of a large statue of an Asian lion, a cityscape behind her in the distance. Hong Kong maybe, perhaps Singapore, Alex wasn't sure. But for a second she could feel the clammy humid air on her arms, could feel the sweat rolling down her back, could smell exotic scents and feel the thrill of a new place to discover.

Of course, she texted back. She missed it so much that it hurt sometimes, so much that she could taste it, the stale air of a plane, the salty tang of a boat. True, the longing was coming less often with time, but it was just as strong when it did come.

Just wait, she told herself. Just wait. You're doing the right thing.

Kat's car pulled into the lot.

Maybe it was time to start planning a summer adventure with Libby. She wasn't too young to travel. Europe might be a good starting place.

Kat got out of her car, her tight skirt and white blouse making Alex's heart skip a beat. Maybe Kat could come too. Maybe they could make a whole summer of it.

She grinned and opened her door. One step at a time though. Now wasn't the time to be making grand gestures.

"Enough about my day. There's only so many screaming kids you can be interested in," Kat said, smiling gently so that a small dimple appeared on her cheek. "What about you? How was your day?" She stirred her coffee.

"Mine?" Alex said. She shrugged. "Boring. Nothing. Cleaned. Shopped. Met the neighbor for coffee and then babysitting."

"Would this be the famous Doug?"

"It would. He's been... helping me."

"With what?" Kat said curiously.

"Trying to find out what I'm going to do with my life," Alex said. She groaned. "That makes me sound like a confused seventeen year old."

Kat laughed. "Not at all, some of us take longer than others to figure things out. What's the problem?"

"I'm just not good at anything," Alex said, cupping her hands around her mug. "I'm not. I've got no experience, no real skills. Doug keeps telling me to make these lists of what I'm good at, what I can do, and I keep coming up blank. Which just makes me think that I can't do a thing."

"That's not true," said Kat. "You've got skills. Valuable ones, actually."

"Right," said Alex. "You're just trying to get into my pants now." Another laugh and Alex wanted to kiss her but knew if she started she wouldn't be able to stop.

"I mean it, Alex. Your organizational skills are top notch. That bake sale was the most efficient, not to mention the most profitable, one I've ever seen. And during School in Nature, when I got hurt, you sprang into action, making sure everyone knew what they were doing and everything was taken care of."

"That's just... Doing stuff," said Alex. "It's not a skill."

"Yes, darling, it really is."

Darling. With a soft little 'k' sound at the end instead of a 'g'. Kat's accent was almost invisible, but every now and again it surfaced and made Alex shudder with desire.

"You're also extremely well traveled," Alex went on. "You know a lot about different cultures and countries, and more importantly about the logistics of being in those places and traveling from one place to another."

"That's a skill?"

Yet another laugh and Alex had to sit on her hands to stop herself reaching out for the woman.

"Everything's a skill if you're able to market it," Kat said. "If I were you, I'd work out where your flair for organization and your lust for travel intersect and go from there."

"Easier said than done."

"Food for thought," Kat said. She drained her cup. "And I really have to go. I have lessons to plan and I don't want to leave you, but I'll never have the energy to keep up with a class of seven year olds if I don't get a good night's sleep."

Alex felt a surge of resentment at that, but swallowed it down. This was Kat's job, what she loved to do. It was important. And she'd known this was only coffee. "Sure thing," she said. "But I get to walk you to your car, right?"

Kat grinned and lifted an eyebrow. "Is that all you're planning on doing? Walking me to my car?"

She watched Kat's tail-lights fade into the distance and shivered a little. It was getting cold, winter was creeping up on them. And her legs were still a little shaky, her lips still a little swollen, her core still a little molten after that goodnight kiss.

It was like being a teenager all over again, she thought, as she leaned up against her car, letting the cool night air brush against her hot cheeks.

They were taking it slow, she got that. She got that Kat was freshly divorced and needed a little time. Her brain understood things. But her body was going insane and screaming at her to just sleep with the woman already.

It was simultaneously frustrating and incredibly hot. She definitely needed a minute before she could get into the car and drive.

Travel and organization. They were interesting points. She'd run them past Doug when she got home, see what he thought.

She bent her neck so that she was looking up at the stars. Pursuing Kat had never been part of the plan, but then, she hadn't really had a plan, had she? It scared her a little that she was settling into this suburban life so quickly. A kid, a house, a potential girlfriend. Commitments, responsibilities. But that didn't detract from how much she wanted Kat, from the growing feelings she had.

Her phone rang again. She pulled it out. Another unknown number.

With a grunt, she opened the car door and threw her phone onto the passenger seat before climbing in. Now wasn't the time for phone calls. She needed to get home. Whatever telemarketer it was would either give up or keep calling until she was bored enough to answer.

She turned the key in the ignition and pulled out of her parking space. The phone didn't stop until she was already back on the road home.

CHAPTER TWENTY TWO

The third date. Fifth if you counted the two times they'd had coffee. Kat knew that she was stretching things out, knew that she needed to make the leap, but it just wasn't happening. She was damned if she knew why, really why. Maybe she was just scared. That was part of it, she was sure, but there was more to it than that.

Alex's phone rang and she turned it over. The second time that evening.

"Not important?" Kat asked.

"Stupid telemarketer," said Alex. "We're playing a game of chicken now. They call, like, five times a day and I don't pick up. At this point, I feel like if I do then I'm losing."

Kat scratched her nose. "You know, most telemarketers don't call at nine in the evening."

"Huh. Yeah. Maybe you're right." Now Alex was looking at her now-silent phone with concern on her face and Kat felt bad.

"Maybe it's some foreign call center," she said, helpfully.

The waitress brought back Alex's credit card. Alex stood and held out her hand to Kat, who took it, feeling that crackle of electricity between them and then getting panicky again. Third date. Third real date. That was when... well, when good girls started to get bad, wasn't it?

"Feel like a walk?" Alex said.

"Maybe."

"Or, you know, you could always come over to my place."

Kat hesitated but knew she couldn't say yes. "Not tonight."

They walked slowly down the sidewalk, still hand in hand but Kat felt that some of the pressure was gone, some of the electricity was being funneled elsewhere.

"You think I'm a bad parent," Alex said.

"What?" In truth, parenting had been the last thing on her mind. Kat had no idea where this had come from.

"You think I'm a bad parent," Alex repeated. "For wanting to bring you home when Libby is there, for, uh, thinking about sex when there's a child around. I get it. Maybe I am being a bad parent. I'm honestly really not sure how this is supposed to go."

"No," Kat said. "No, not at all. I wasn't thinking that or anything like it."

"But you won't come back with me."

Kat stopped walking. "No," she said softly. "I want to, I truly do. I like you a lot, Alex. I desire you. But... I don't know, it's me, not you, I swear."

Alex raised an eyebrow and the sparkle in her blue eyes made Kat want to kiss her. "That old chestnut."

"I just mean... I haven't. Since the divorce. And, um, even before that, there was only one woman before Jen, my ex-wife. So I'm not exactly experienced. And... I don't even know if I can explain it. It just doesn't feel right yet."

And, and said a voice in her head, what if this is all there is? What if all this, the dinners, the conversations, the company, is all based on electric desire and once you release all that pent up energy there's nothing else left? She wasn't sure she was strong enough to deal with that, another break up, so soon.

"Okay," Alex said slowly. They'd walked around the block nearly, and Kat could see her car. "I guess I can understand that. But... I want you to know that I don't want to wait."

"Okay," Kat said, feeling ice in her stomach. Was this it? Was she getting dumped anyway?

"You're a little old-fashioned," Alex said. "I'm not like that. I'm trying to understand. But, well, I can't help but think that maybe this isn't what you want."

They walked a little further and were close enough to touch Alex's car and Kat didn't know what to say. She knew what Alex meant. Old-fashioned. That was code for boring. She was boring and Alex was getting bored waiting for her. She could taste metal in her mouth and didn't know what to say.

"I guess I'll go then," Alex said. She turned. "You sure you don't want to come with me?"

It had nothing to do with want. She wanted to go. She couldn't. It just... didn't seem right yet. No matter how boring and staid that was. And if Alex thought she was boring, really boring, then maybe she should just leave, because Kat didn't see herself getting more exciting overnight. She didn't know what to do. She shook her head.

Alex leaned over and brushed a kiss on her cheek. Then she opened her car door and got in, starting the engine and driving off without looking back.

Kat's fragile heart cracked a little. Of course it had come to this. It had to come to this. She'd known from the beginning that she wasn't interesting enough, modern enough for Alex.

"Come, talk to me!"

Fran's voice came from the living room as Kat shut the front door. She was in no mood to talk, but she couldn't turn down Fran, not after all she'd done. She appeared in the living room doorway and saw Fran lying on the couch.

"My date was disastrous," Fran said. "All he could talk about was golf. I hope yours was better. Come, sit down, I just opened a bottle, get yourself a glass."

Actually, a glass of wine was just what she needed to help her sleep. She grabbed a glass and poured some.

"Well, what are you going to do about the job?" Fran said as

Kat sat down.

Jesus, the job, she'd almost forgotten about it in the thrill of seeing Alex. "I don't know," she said honestly.

"It's a good offer," Fran said. "And they're not going to wait forever for an answer."

Kat closed her eyes and leaned her head back against the couch. A year ago, just a year ago, her life had been so perfect. Teaching, married, in a house of her own. Yet here she was, homeless, unable to take the next step with a woman she thought she liked, and contemplating changing her career.

"You shouldn't take it," Fran said.

"What?" Kat opened her eyes.

"I can see how hard this is for you," Fran said with a sympathetic look. "It's tearing you apart thinking about leaving your classroom. If it's that hard, you shouldn't take the job. We'll find another way to do things, another way to help you."

We. We'll find. Fran had always been there, always helped. It was time to stop taking advantage of her. Kat patted her knee.

"It's not that. I'm still thinking about the job, honestly. I haven't decided yet. I'm just down because..."

"Ah, because of this new woman." Fran struggled to sit up and then poured more wine in her glass. "You know, if you'd let me meet her then I could give you a full evaluation on what I think."

Kat laughed. "I'm not sure I'm ready for that yet."

"What's the problem, babe?"

"I'm boring. That's what it is. She's so interesting and exciting and different, and I, well, I can't even persuade myself that I should, um, you know, with her. Even though I really want to."

Fran bit back a smile and shook her head. "My dear, you're not boring. I know what you think, and I know what Jen did to you, but you're far from boring. Okay, you're not the bungee jumping type, but you've read books I've never even heard of. You're a first generation immigrant. That's not boring. And if this girl is pressuring you because you won't have sex with her then—"

"No, she's not pressuring me," Kat said quickly. Or at least she didn't think she was. Alex's goodbye hadn't exactly been warm.

"This is on me, not on her."

Fran took her hand and squeezed it. "In that case, then don't be so hard on yourself. You're entire life got swung upside down in the last year, you have good reason to be cautious, good reason to take your time. I think it's great that you're dating again, but don't run before you can walk. You do you."

Kat sipped at her wine. It made sense. She still wished she could see more clearly, that she could pinpoint where the problem was. But maybe it wasn't going to matter. Alex had just driven off. Maybe she was only going to see her at awkward parent-teacher conferences from now on. Maybe she'd already bored her away.

The phone rang just as she got out of the shower. She picked it up without thinking. To call this late must mean some kind of emergency.

"It's me."

Alex's voice settled some of the storm in her head. "Hi."

"Listen, I was a bitch tonight. Just driving off like that. I was frustrated."

"It's fine, I—"

"No, let me finish. I've had time to think. I need to be less spontaneous, to think about you more. This must be so hard for you, and maybe I don't really understand as much as I want to because I've never been in your situation before."

There was a pause and Kat could hear Alex taking a breath.

"I was thinking about what you said, about it not feeling right yet. And that's fine. Totally fine. But maybe it's something I could help a little with. On Saturday the house will be empty. Libby's going to a sleepover. Would you like to come to my place for dinner?"

"I—"

"No, still not done," Alex said and Kat grinned. "There's no expectations, nothing, I promise you. I just thought that maybe if we had some privacy, maybe if you could come over without

Libby being here, some of the pressure might be off. I'm willing to wait for you as long as you want, I swear I am. And I swear I won't get all handsy or grabby or anything. I just want to have dinner with you and somewhere we can be alone and quiet and —"

"Yes," interrupted Kat, grinning so hard her face was starting to hurt. "Yes, just stop talking. You don't need to convince me. Yes, I'd love to come and have dinner with you."

She could sense the relief over the phone.

"Thank you," Alex said. There was another pause. Then a small voice said: "I think I like you more than I planned, Ms. Stein."

Kat's stomach did a flip. "The feeling's mutual," she whispered.

CHAPTER TWENTY THREE

I like you more than I planned. What the hell was wrong with her? The words had been spinning around her head all week, echoing as she waved Libby off to her sleepover. It wasn't exactly the most romantic thing to say. It was true, she had that going for her. But just because something was true didn't mean that it needed saying.

She straightened a pillow on the couch and angled the coasters a little more. Look at her. Just look at her. Straightening up like the queen was coming for tea. Like how her house looked was the most important thing about tonight.

Alex let herself fall into one of the armchairs. What had she turned into? One woman, a handful of kisses, and suddenly she was practically Martha Stewart. She just... she wanted to impress Kat, wanted to show that she was reliable, a good parent, something like that. It still worried her, deep down, that Kat was judging her, and that she was coming up short.

If she'd only met Kat in a beach bar on an island somewhere. They could have had their fun already. But then... but then she'd have run away, just like she always did. She'd have skipped town and moved onto the next place, the next woman.

That wasn't a possibility now. Not with Libby in tow. And that thought scared her, terrified her. But there was something that frightened her even more. The thought that the obvious chemistry between them was all there was. What if they went to bed and then in the morning the feelings were gone?

In her old life, she'd sneak out with her shoes in her hand. But it was becoming rapidly clear that Kat in no way fit in with her old life.

A savory, meaty smell wafted from the kitchen.

"Fuck."

She made it to the oven just in time. The lasagna was a little browner than the picture on the website but still looked edible. Alex looked down at it. She'd cooked. Just how far was she willing to go for Kat?

On the counter, her phone started to ring and she moved to pick it up just as the doorbell sounded. Screw it. She stood up straight, swallowed, took a deep breath and marched to the front door.

"What about your entrepreneurial plans, how are they going?" asked Kat, stabbing some salad with her fork.

"A bit stalled," Alex said. Honestly, she'd spent so much time thinking about Kat that she had worked little on anything else. She had the beginning of an idea, but she was far from ready to announce it. "But you helped, you telling me that I had skills, it was helpful, thank you."

Kat blushed a little and sighed. "You're not the only one with career problems."

"I'm not?" The lasagna was better than she'd expected, she was kind of proud of herself.

"Eh, I got offered a corporate job."

"You?" Alex said, wine glass halfway to her mouth. "Not that you shouldn't get a corporate job, just... you seem like the perfect teacher, that's all."

"Not perfect. But it is what I've always wanted to do. I guess life gets in the way sometimes."

"Tell me about it," Alex said. "We can't always have what we want. Still though, I find it hard to imagine you not teaching."

Kat smiled. "So do I."

"If, uh, if there's anything I can do to help?"

"Thanks for the offer, but I just need a little time to think about things, that's all," Kat said. She placed her knife and fork side by side on her plate. "And that was delicious."

Alex cleared her throat. They'd fallen easily into conversation, there was never any weirdness when it was just the two of them, as long as they weren't discussing Libby or child-rearing or school. But there was still a pall over the evening, a sense of something unfinished, and she wanted to be clear.

"Kat, I wanted to say that I appreciate you coming over here. And also, well, also I think you're brave to be dating again. It must be exceptionally difficult and I don't appreciate how tough it is."

"It's strange," Kat said with a small smile. Her hair was down and she tucked a lock of it behind her ear.

"Right," Alex said. "Um, a while ago, the first time we went out, I told you that I'd wait. I just wanted you to know that that still holds. I like you a lot, but I'll wait as long as you need, Kat. I was wrong to infer that I wouldn't."

Kat was standing up now and Alex took her cue, collecting the plates and the silverware.

"It's nice of you to say," Kat said.

Alex just nodded and took the plates to the sink, running the faucet over them. Outside the night was black and she could see the reflection of Kat coming up behind her, could smell her perfume full of flowers, and then feel her warmth.

Kat leaned in, her lips almost brushing Alex's ear. "But I don't want you to wait any longer."

Alex's hands froze, the faucet still running until Kat reached around her and turned it off. She took a breath. "Do you mean that?"

"I do," Kat said. "It feels right now, I don't know how or why, it just does. I feel ready. Just…"

Alex turned around so that they were facing each other, so that she could see Kat looking down at the floor. "Just what?" she asked.

"Just... Be gentle. I feel like this is the first time, I'm afraid of making a mistake, I'm scared that... I don't know, that I won't know what to do anymore." Kat's face was flushing.

"I don't think you need to worry about that," Alex said. She cupped Kat's face in her hand, tilted her chin a little so that they were eye to eye. "It's like riding a bike."

Kat smiled and pulled in, her lips so close to Alex's that she felt the words as much as heard them. "You're nothing like a bike, darling, trust me on that."

A hand was on her waist already and Alex felt her legs start to tremble. What was this? She'd never been so nervous, never so on edge. It was Kat that closed the kiss, that pulled her in softly so that their lips met and Alex sank into her.

For a long moment that was all there was. The kiss, Kat's lips and tongue, the softness of her skin, the warmth of her body, and the steady dripping of the faucet behind them. For a long moment that was all Alex needed or wanted and she would die happy just from this. For a long moment there was no need to hurry, even desire was on pause for as long as it took for the perfect kiss to happen.

Then Alex's phone rang again.

In her haste she pushed it off the counter, hearing it clatter onto the floor as she pulled Kat into her, hopping up onto the counter and parting her legs, getting Kat as close as she could be before wrapping her legs around her waist and twisting her hands into that golden hair.

"I need you."

She wasn't entirely sure who had said the words but she didn't care, it honestly didn't matter. Until Kat pulled away.

"Wait," she said.

Immediately, Alex stopped. "Too fast?"

"No, not fast enough," Kat said, her breath coming quickly. "But not here. Upstairs."

The crispness of her accent was stronger now, she was less in control of herself and even the hint of Kat being out of control turned Alex into a molten ball of desire. She jumped from the counter, took Kat by both hands and pulled at her.

"Come."

Obediently, Kat followed her up the stairs. Alex was half-running as though afraid that her desire would start without her. She could feel her heartbeat between her legs and she was shaking with need.

They crashed into the bedroom, Alex pulling Kat in to kiss her again, running her hands over that slim body, desperate now to get to her skin, to reveal her breasts, to slide down her underwear, to…

"Take off your shirt."

Kat's voice was a little harder now, strained with want. Alex took a step back and pulled her t-shirt over her head revealing her bare torso.

"And your pants."

She shimmied them down, letting Kat take control, knowing that she needed to do this. She stood naked and unashamed, letting Kat's eyes rove over her body. Only when Kat's gaze returned to her own did she move.

Her fingers reached for the zipper of Kat's skirt, sliding it down until the garment pooled around her feet. Shaking, she steadily unbuttoned Kat's blouse, the buttons popping from the button-holes with agonizing slowness.

Then Kat was standing there, black underwear against porcelain white skin, heat and desire radiating off her and Alex groaned.

"I can't wait anymore."

Kat smiled and Alex saw the promise in that smile and almost fainted as her pulse sky-rocketed.

"No more waiting," Kat agreed.

CHAPTER TWENTY FOUR

The light of the bedroom was soft and dim, caressing the curves of the body in front of her. Alex was lithe, thin, muscles stringing along her arms and legs, and strongly, defiantly naked. As though she was daring Kat to touch her, to take her.

Kat had had her moment of power, she'd forced Alex to undress, but now that she was staring at her, now that Alex was live and real in front of her, she found that she couldn't move. She was afraid, afraid of breaking her, of breaking herself, afraid of what came next.

The bedroom smelled of coconut and something that was uniquely Alex. No more waiting, she'd said. No more waiting but here she was, waiting.

Alex put out her hand and Kat took it.

"Slowly," Alex said. "Slowly. It's okay."

Suddenly, this was what she needed. After the heat of desire, the desperate clutching need to touch and kiss and be kissed, she needed a moment, a calmness, a gentleness. She followed Alex's lead, allowing herself to be lowered onto the bed. She could feel Alex's eyes on her as though those eyes were hands, stroking down her body. She felt herself flush and respond.

"Let me," Alex said softly.

Real hands this time, brushing against her skin and raising goosebumps so that Kat shivered and her mouth started to water with wanting.

"It's all going to be fine," said Alex. "Trust me."

And she did. She trusted Alex to take care of her, to help her take this big step. And when Alex's hand brushed over her nipple, she gasped. And when Alex's hand stroked down her thigh, she moaned. And when Alex's hand parted her legs, she let it happen.

There was a darkness in Alex's deep blue eyes as her fingers searched and found what they were looking for. Kat stifled a moan as Alex dipped into her slickness.

"Trust me," Alex said again.

Kat forced herself to relax, forced her breathing to be even. And Alex's fingers slowly began to circle around her center, dipping in and out of her wetness as Kat's pulse started to quicken.

She twitched, licking her lips, feeling the pressure building inside her. She began to pull away, wanting it to last, not wanting her climax yet. But Alex stopped her, pressed harder.

"Just let it happen," she whispered. "Just take this step with me."

Alex lay herself down so that she was pressed against Kat's side, so that Kat could feel her warmth and smell her scent and hear her breathing. And those fingers worked again and Kat closed her eyes and let herself disappear into the feeling.

She didn't stop it, that steadily growing explosion inside her. She didn't control it or force herself in any way. Instead, she let her legs open and let Alex's fingers work and then slowly, slowly, fell over the edge into a chasm of pulsing waves.

After, she opened her eyes and smiled and breathed and it was as though something inside had been lifted, shackles had been taken off, something changed. Because now when she looked at Alex, smiling down at her, all she wanted was to take her.

No shame, no regret, no baggage, no nothing. The step had been taken, Alex had helped her, and now, now the dam had been opened and Kat felt nothing more than raw desire.

Turning, she pushed Alex back onto the bed.

"You don't have to..." began Alex.

"Yes," said Kat, passion hard in her voice. "Yes, I do. I need to."

She bent and suckled Alex's breasts until her nipples were standing up in hard points and already she could feel Alex squirming beneath her, could feel her hips moving, desperate for contact. As she'd promised she had absolutely no intention of making the woman wait. Not anymore.

She slid her tongue down Alex's tight stomach felt rather than heard the gasp as she forced herself between Alex's legs. The smell of desire was deep and musky and Kat was already swelling again, already feeling wetness.

"Jesus, Kat," Alex groaned as Kat kissed up the inside of her thighs.

Kat's kisses turned to nibbles and the smell of Alex was filling her up and screw Alex not waiting, it was Kat now that didn't want to wait.

There was nothing gentle about it, there was no teasing or tickling. She pushed her head between Alex's legs, got her first taste of citrus and musk, licked at the swollen, delicate tissue surrounding her center, and then went straight to the point.

"Ah, please," moaned Alex.

And the words just spurred her on. Alex pushed up to her tongue, increasing the pressure. Kat could feel slickness on her cheeks as Alex's wetness spilled over onto her thighs, mixing with her own saliva, making everything slide and glide together as she rocked in motion with Alex's hips.

"Just like that," Alex gasped.

Kat changed nothing, letting her tongue do the work, feeling Alex's thighs begin to shake and then hearing her moans change pitch. She felt the contractions as Alex pushed up against her and felt her own wetness running down the inside of her thighs.

Jesus, she needed this.

She waited just long enough for Alex to come down, for her breathing to equalize, for her thigh muscles to relax again.

Then she climbed back up on the bed, sitting astride her,

holding down Alex's arms and looking deep into those blue eyes. Alex's cheeks were red, her hair was sticking up and Kat had never before seen anything so sexy. She bent and kissed her, long and hard, letting Alex taste herself on her lips. She ground her hips against Alex's stomach, letting her wetness flow between them, lubricating herself.

It was almost enough, but not quite. She felt the pressure building again and moaned into Alex's mouth.

And then she could take no more.

She released one of Alex's hands, bringing the other toward her, pushing the fingers together so that she could fill herself with them.

"Fuck me."

It was the first time she'd ever said that. Make love to me, sure, take me, okay. But not fuck. That was exactly what she wanted though, what she needed.

Alex's fingers plunged inside her and Kat fingered her own clit feeling the heat building up inside her hard and fast as she rode Alex's hand. She bucked once, twice, and then squeezed herself against Alex's long, strong fingers and let out a yell that sounded unearthly.

Blackness came over her, stars and explosions and all the trite things that were supposed to happen. But she saw none of it. She was lost in a world of sensation that she'd never been to before.

When finally she fell to the bed, gasping and panting and still contracting inside, breathless and almost crying from the intensity of it all, Alex wrapped her in her arms.

"Thank you," she managed to say.

"Thank you," whispered Alex, pulling her in closer.

"I... it's never, I've never..."

"Shh," said Alex. "We're not done yet."

Kat laughed then, the sound really bringing her back to earth. "We're not?" she asked, still a little breathless.

"Unless you want to be?" asked Alex anxiously.

Those blue eyes looked into hers and Kat's heart skipped a beat. She didn't want to be. She didn't ever want to be done with this. With Alex. With whatever this was. She'd been so afraid there'd be nothing once the sexual tension had been broken. Yet the feelings were still there, even stronger than before.

"I don't want to be," she said. "I could stay here forever."

"Be my guest," Alex said with a grin.

The clock by the bed was flashing eight-oh-five when the doorbell rang. Kat glanced at it, then looked back at Alex, who was sleepily snuggled in her arms. The bell rang again and Alex opened one eye.

"Who the hell could that be at this time on a Sunday?"

"There's only one way to find out," Kat said, as loathe as she was to let Alex leave her arms.

Alex struggled up and pulled on some yoga pants and a t-shirt, hair sticking up in eight different directions. She padded out of the bedroom and Kat stretched. She was awake now. And... probably they should have some sustenance before maybe taking advantage of an empty house and a quiet Sunday morning. She grinned to herself, got up, and found a robe on the back of the bathroom door.

She was at the top of the stairs when she saw the tall, dark-haired man framed by the front door.

She was half way down the stairs before she realized what he had said.

She made it to the bottom just in time to catch Alex's arm and stop her slamming the door.

Alex looked at her, looked back at the man, then looked at Kat again, fear and pain and desperation turning her eyes into stormy lakes.

"Kat," she said. "This..." She swallowed, licked her lips, then tried again. "This is Libby's father."

CHAPTER TWENTY FIVE

Alex stood back and let Kat do the work, ushering the man inside, sitting him in the living room. Her mouth was too dry to speak, her heart too cracked to let herself speak. Her head felt like it was filled with cotton wool as Kat's hand gently steered her into an armchair.

"I'll get some coffee," Kat said.

And Alex was left alone with him. As though struck by a sudden idea she searched his face, looking for signs that he wasn't who he said he was. But she could see it. She could see the curve of his cheekbone, the slant of his eye, the angle of his hairline. Her hand twitched, the hand that stroked Libby's hair as she fell asleep.

"I, uh, realize this must be a surprise," the man said.

He was tall and dark-haired and not unattractive. And from his tone, was just as uncomfortable as Alex was. "Yes," she allowed.

"I did try to call," he said. "I tried to call many times but… Maybe I was given the wrong number, I don't know."

All those fucking telemarketing calls. Alex swallowed and took a breath. He was sitting right there, sitting in her living room. And she was afraid to talk to him.

"Coffee," Kat announced, bringing in a tray.

Alex grasped at a cup, grateful to give her hands something to do. The man hesitated before he took one for himself.

"Alistair Huston," he said for Kat's benefit.

Kat arched an eyebrow and sat down close enough that Alex could reach out and touch her if she needed to. Alex wanted her right there, wanted to feel her, draw warmth from her. She was pathetically grateful to have someone by her side.

"Why don't you tell us what's going on here?" Kat said.

The man shrugged. "I wish I knew. I'm Olivia's father. Her mother and I, well, it's complicated. Claire told me she was pregnant just as I was moving to Hong Kong. She insisted that she do this alone, that she wanted nothing from me. I was... To tell you the truth, I was shocked. I ran away."

Something she could understand, Alex thought. But then at least he'd had the chance to run away, which was more than she'd had.

"I came back to the country about six months ago. Found out about Claire, and then spent plenty of time trying to track down my daughter."

My daughter. As though he had a claim to her. Alex's hands tightened around her mug. She looked to Kat.

"And what do you want?" Kat asked sharply.

Alex could hear the school teacher in her tone and almost smiled.

Alistair sighed before putting down his coffee cup. "I want my daughter back," he said.

She didn't know she'd done it until she heard the crash. Coffee dripped down the side of the armchair, shattered porcelain lay on the ground and Alex's hands were empty. Kat was standing already, Alistair staring at her open-mouthed.

"I think it would be best if you left," Kat said grimly.

She was taking him by the elbow, escorting him out, exchanging quiet words with him before the door slammed shut behind him and then she was pulling Alex out of her chair and cradling her.

"It's going to be okay."

"It's not," Alex said, her face drained and her whole body shaking. "It's not going to be okay. He wants Libby, he…"

"It's a shock," said Kat. "I get that. But try and stay calm. There are processes for this kind of thing. He can't just take her. Alex, please, listen to me, this is going to be okay."

And Alex desperately wanted to believe her.

The lawyer sniffed and ran his tongue over his teeth. Alex could smell the sharp spike of his cologne. Next to her, Doug held tightly onto her hand. Kat was at school, but Doug had fallen over himself trying to help her. He'd driven her here as well as done most of the talking.

"So, where do we go from here?" Doug asked now.

"First things first, we demand a paternity test," the lawyer said. "That's par for the course. No point in fighting or discussing anything if he's not the actual father."

"And assuming he is?" Doug asked.

"Then we start trying to come to an arrangement. There'll initially be some negotiation, we do our best to try and keep child custody cases out of the court room. There'll be an independent investigation into the child's welfare."

"What does that mean?" Alex broke in.

The lawyer sniffed again. "Interviews with school teachers, psychologists where necessary, a look around the child's environment, nothing for you to be worried about, Ms. Blakely."

"Then what?" Doug asked.

"Then we sit down and agree with the other party about who has the child and when, or we take the whole thing in front of a judge and let him decide," the lawyer said. He leaned forward in his chair. "I'm not going to lie to you, Ms. Blakely. Child custody issues are rarely pleasant, a lot of dirty laundry gets aired and emotions get high. It's in everyone's best interest that you're sure this is what you want to do, and that you're sure there are no other options."

Alex nodded obediently.

Ever since the knock on the door, ever since Alistair Huston had appeared, she'd felt like she was walking around in a cloud, the world dull and quiet around her, her own thoughts and feelings too loud. Kat had comforted her, and when she'd left, Libby had come home and Alex had held her and tried not to scare her and told her nothing. She didn't know what to tell her.

Doug wrapped things up, took Alex's arm, got her back to the car. Only when they were sitting in the car, the air cold around them, did Alex take a deep gulping breath and blink the tears away.

"Are you okay?" Doug asked. "Strike that, I know you're not. But is there something you need?"

"I need all of this to go away," Alex said.

Doug laughed. "I hear you."

He was quiet for a moment. Quiet enough that Alex turned to him. "Are you okay?" she asked.

He looked at her with clear blue eyes. "Alex, I have to ask this. I've been involved in custody cases before, and anyone that gets dragged into these things knows how hateful they can get. Are you really sure you want to fight this?"

Alex looked down at her hands, twisting a tissue between her fingers. She couldn't blame him for asking, she'd had similar thoughts herself.

"Six months ago, hell, three months ago, I'd have said no," she said. "I'd have been relieved, to be honest, that Libby had another responsible adult to depend on."

"Nobody's going to think badly of you if you choose to let Libby go to her father," said Doug.

"Yes they will," Alex said. "I will. Because..." Her eyes filled with tears again and she had to pause to blink them away. "Because as much as I couldn't imagine my life as a parent before, now I can't imagine my life without her. She's a little girl, Doug. I can't just hand her over to a stranger. But it's more than that, I don't want to hand her over to a stranger. I might not be the best mother on the planet, but I love her."

Doug smiled and nodded. "I know you do," he said. "But I had to ask, Alex."

"This is the right thing to do," Alex said, still looking at her hands. "It's the right thing to do but that's not why I'm doing it. I'm doing it because it's the thing I want to do."

"In that case, I'm here for you every step of the way," Doug said starting the engine.

On the drive home, Alex watched out of the window. Houses flowed past, houses with families and children inside them. She'd changed. The last few months had changed her. She wasn't who she used to be. Slowly, incrementally, she'd become more settled, happier. Some of that had to do with Kat. Most of that had to do with Libby.

She pulled out her phone and clicked open her messages. Evie's picture of the sun-soaked beach stared back at her. For once, she had no longing to be there.

The only place she wanted to be was here, with Libby. And... if she really thought about it, with Kat too.

A little family all of their own.

A little family that she didn't even know if Kat wanted, but suspected that she did.

A little family that was now threatened.

The lump in her throat grew larger and a tear escaped, sliding down the side of her face.

CHAPTER TWENTY SIX

It was hard to keep her hands off Alex. The memory of their night together was still fresh and strong, and Kat was still processing her feelings about it. But she knew one thing for sure, she didn't want that to be their only night together.

But Alex in her classroom wasn't Alex. She was Ms. Blakely, and Kat restrained herself. She felt a rush of warmth to her stomach, but her voice was steady as she greeted Alex.

"Is there something I can do for you, Ms. Blakely?" Kat said.

There was a ghost of a smile on Alex's face. "All professional at school are we?" she said. The glint in her eye came and went and her smile dropped. "I saw the lawyer."

Kat nodded. Olivia wasn't the first kid to go through a custody battle in her class, she knew how these things went. She also knew that she had to be extremely careful to separate the personal and the professional. "Right, you'll need an assessment, I'm guessing?"

Alex nodded. "If you wouldn't mind. It's important to me that we get this over and done with as quickly as possible. I've got all the paperwork."

"I've done this before," Kat said.

She took a deep breath. This wasn't going to be easy.

"Um, Ms. Blakely. Alex. I, uh, I have to say that this is my job.

At least for the time being."

Alex frowned. "And?"

"And I'm happy to fill out the assessment for Olivia's custody hearing. But I will be completely honest. I have to be completely honest. You know that, right? I'm only telling you in case you see the assessment later. I can't let my personal feelings about you affect my job."

It sounded stilted and strange and Alex's face clouded and Kat wanted nothing more than to take her in her arms and hold her. But to give her her due, Alex nodded again. "I get it. I understand." There was a time, Kat thought, not so long ago, when Alex would have jumped all over her for saying something like that, when they'd have fought and yelled.

"I don't think there's anything terrible that I have to say," Kat said, smiling now. "But I'll probably be interviewed at some point, and I don't know what questions will be asked, so I can't tell you a hundred percent what my replies will be."

"But you don't think I'm a bad parent."

Kat hesitated for a millisecond before she shook her head. "I don't."

She didn't. Not really. Though what was best in this particular circumstance she had no idea. Alex had given up everything to care for Olivia, but it must have been hard. And it could be a decision she would regret later, she might long after her old life. Alistair Huston was Olivia's biological father, was it right to keep him away from his daughter?

Kat was glad she wasn't the one having to decide anything.

"Thank you," Alex said quietly. "That means a lot."

And now Kat did break her rules. She couldn't help herself. Alex looked so lost, so sad, that she had to go to her, to hold her. She pressed Alex's warmth against her.

"It's going to be okay," she said.

And she wished she could believe that. But she'd seen too many parental divorces to swear that this would all have a happy ending.

"You've got, like, two weeks to decide," Fran said. She was still in her running gear, stretching out in the kitchen, sweating and gleaming.

"I know that," said Kat, putting down her cup of tea. "But I haven't decided yet. I want the job, I think. But then I walk into the classroom and... And I can't imagine myself doing anything else."

"Then you need to turn it down. Give Jackson a chance to find someone else to fill the position."

"I know, I know," Kat said. "And you need to go jump in the shower, you smell horrific."

"There's nothing wrong with the smell of hard work," Fran said with a grin. But she jogged off toward her bathroom anyway.

Kat picked up her tea again and went back to staring through the kitchen window. It was dark outside, the evenings closed in early at this time of year. It had been a long day. She'd filled in the assessment for Olivia Blakely during lunch and mailed it on her way home.

And now all she could think about was Alex. She should be thinking about the future, about a job, about a place of her own, a healthier bank account. But every time she tried to concentrate she ended up thinking about Alex instead. Alex and Olivia, who was such a charming little girl, about Alex's house, how that should have been the life she had. A woman she loved, a child to dote on, and a house to fill with happiness.

That was all she'd ever wanted.

She couldn't tell Alex that though. She couldn't tell her that after just a few weeks, after a grand total of one night together, she was already thinking about moving in, about building something, about...

The feelings were there. She'd fallen in love before, she knew what was happening. She knew that she was falling for Alex Blakely and that somehow, magically, Alex seemed to be responding to her. And to think she'd hated the woman at first sight.

She smiled a little and her reflection looked sad.

"Penny for your thoughts."

Kat turned around.

"Forgot my water bottle," Fran said, picking up the offending item. "And you looked... sad. Having a bad day?"

"No, not really. A long day. I was just... thinking."

"Too much thinking is dangerous," said Fran, stepping in closer. "What's up?"

Kat sighed. "Alex."

"Ah, the mysterious Alex. I thought things were going well there?"

"They are," said Kat. "Or at least I think they are." She hadn't seen Alex for almost a week, since she'd dropped by the school. But it was understandable that currently Alex was a little distracted by other things. "Perhaps a little too well."

"What on earth does that mean?" Fran laughed. Then she stopped and her eyes widened. "Katarina Stein, are you falling in love with the woman?"

Kat felt herself blush and could do nothing other than nod.

"Then you have to tell her," Fran said, coming closer. "And I have to meet her."

Panic fluttered in Kat's stomach. "I can't do that."

Fran rolled her eyes and opened the fridge, pulling out a half full bottle of wine. She poured some into two glasses and handed one to Kat. "I can shower later, and you look like you need alcohol. This conversation feels like it needs alcohol," she said by way of explanation. "Now why can't you tell the woman you have feelings for her."

"Because she's about to start a custody battle for her daughter and she has more important things to worry about than me."

"Or, she would welcome the support from someone who loves her," countered Fran.

"Because we've only known each other for a few weeks."

"Which is more than long enough to figure whether you actually like someone or not," Fran said. "Unless you're particularly indecisive, which you're not."

"Because..." Kat sighed again. "Because I'm worried that she thinks I'm boring. And if I tell her I have feelings for her then... Then what? A suburban house with kids and vacations at Disneyland? There's no way she'll want that."

"No one's sentencing you to that," Fran said with a shudder. "But from everything you've said about Alex, she's starting to settle down a little. Building a relationship is part of that, surely."

"Maybe. But it'll still come off as boring," Kat said.

"Will it though?" asked Fran with a cocked eyebrow. "Or will it come off as daring and exciting? Because you've only known each other a few weeks and you're jumping in with both feet? That doesn't seem boring to me. Plus, my bet is that if she's lived the life you say she has then she's probably not been in the position of having someone declare serious feelings for her. Which makes it even more exciting."

"Do you really think that?"

Fran grinned. "I don't know. But then, neither do you. You're right, it might go badly. Or it might not. I do know that keeping something like this to yourself isn't fair. You have to give the other party an opportunity to put their case forward, to decide what they want."

"Right."

"And I know you, Kat," Fran said, taking her hand and squeezing it. "I know that you're honest and true and generous. And that if you're falling in love with this woman then she must be something pretty special. So give her a chance. Be daring for once."

Kat drank a mouthful of wine. Fran was right. She should stake her claim, be honest. She didn't know where things were going with Alex, but it was only fair to let her know that there were feelings involved. It might simply give her the chance to escape and run away. Or it might end up with something more. Something bigger and better than she'd ever had before.

Be daring. Be romantic. Kat started to warm to the idea. She'd book a table at a nice restaurant, she could just about stretch her budget to that. Invite Alex to dinner. Not on a school night, she wanted plenty of time to talk about things. So next weekend it would be then. A Friday night, she thought.

She was grinning as she drained her glass of wine. She was really going to do this.

"That's my girl," Fran said, as she finished her own wine and put the glass down. "Go get 'em, tiger."

Kat laughed.

CHAPTER TWENTY SEVEN

"Go on out and have a good time," Doug said. "Me and Libby will be just fine here."

"I don't know, Doug, I just..."

She peeked through to the living room. She'd told Libby three days ago now about her father and the kid wasn't taking it well. It was less the fact that she had a father, which she'd initially been quite excited about, and more the fact that she might have to live with him that was the problem.

"Go," Doug said now. "It's important that you have your own life too, and that you have a little time away from things here."

"I'm not going to be any fun." But secretly her heart was jumping at the idea of seeing Kat. As wrong as it seemed, she couldn't get the woman off her mind. When she dropped into bed in the evening it was Kat that she found herself thinking about.

Doug held her by the shoulders so that he was looking directly at her. "This is all going to be fine," he said. "The courts, the lawyers, the social workers, they're not idiots. It's clearly better to keep Libby with you than it is to send her to some man she doesn't know. Okay, maybe you'll have to share custody, but there's nothing wrong with that, Alex."

"I guess." She didn't want to share Libby, not now. But if that meant that she didn't have to give her up, then she'd do it.

"All the reports should be in by the end of next week or so, then the lawyers can get started. In the meantime, go out, have a drink or two, and have a nice time. And, um..." He blushed a little here. "If you need me to stay here overnight, then that's just fine. I can sleep on the couch."

Alex rolled her eyes, but noted down the fact that he was willing to stay. A night in Kat's arms might be just what she needed.

Kat was just what she needed, she thought as she got into the car. There were definitely feelings there, feelings that she definitely wanted to explore. Okay, she needed to deal with Libby first. But once that was settled, well, she was a hundred percent certain that she wanted to pursue whatever was starting with Kat. It felt weird, weird to want something certain, to feel like building something instead of just taking what was there and running. But it felt right.

She was just pulling in to the parking lot of the restaurant when her phone rang. She answered it, wondering as she did at the fanciness of the place. She could see candles on tables through the window. Kat was going all out on this date, she thought. A place inside her warmed up. Clearly, Kat was also having some feelings, feelings they could explore together...

"Alex Blakely," she said with a grin as she answered the phone.

"Ms. Blakely, it's Lex Foreman here. I know it's late, but I've just heard from the social worker involved in your case."

It got suddenly cold in the car. "Okay," Alex said slowly. The lawyer was brisk, his tone clipped.

"I'm afraid there's been a small set back. The department of child services is insisting on another home visit and interview."

"But they were just here last week," Alex said.

There was a short silence. "Yes," the lawyer said. "But now they want another opportunity to talk to both you and Olivia and to oversee your living situation."

"Why?"

The silence was a little longer this time. "It, uh, it seems that they weren't happy with one of the assessments that was turned in." Foreman cleared his throat. "Someone, and I haven't seen these assessments myself yet so I don't know who, but someone has intimated that perhaps you are not the most suitable guardian for the child. Now—"

"Who the hell would say that?" Alex exploded.

"Ms. Blakely. These things happen. I'm sure it's just a small hiccup, all you need to do is play along and go through with the second interview and everything will be fine. Sometimes the authorities just need a little extra reassurance."

"Reassurance, my ass," Alex said, seeing red now. "Someone thinks I'm a bad parent, someone thinks I can't do this. You need to find out who in hell would say something like that."

"Ms. Blakely, I can't—"

But even as he was speaking, Alex saw Kat's car drive up. She saw Kat inside. She remembered every conversation they'd had. She remembered Kat telling her that Libby's dresses were inappropriate. She remembered Kat telling her that she had to be honest in her assessment. And her blood started to boil.

She hung up the phone, tossing it onto the passenger seat and practically leaping from her car.

"How dare you."

Kat was climbing out of the driver's seat, straightening her skirt. The same skirt she'd been wearing the first time they met, Alex thought. And she remembered that day, remembered Libby's pale little face, remembered the welling of hatred she'd had at anyone that could make her little girl feel that way. Remembered how Kat hadn't called Libby by her nickname, how she'd demanded apologies and... And she clenched her hands into fists.

"How fucking dare you."

"What? Alex? What's going on?"

Kat was walking toward her and Alex was wrenching deep, tearing breaths from her lungs, ready to fly at the woman, ready to scratch out her eyes.

"How dare you," she said again.

"How dare I what?" Kat was close enough to touch now, close

enough that Alex could spit at her.

"You judgmental, interfering, hypocritical bitch."

"Alex—"

"Don't you 'Alex' me. You've never thought I was good enough. From the very beginning you've rolled your eyes at everything I've done, from the clothes I put Libby in to the fact that she calls me by my first name. Nothing I've ever done has been up to scratch for you."

"Alex—" Kat took a step back. "Ms. Blakely." She blinked as though the name was unfamiliar on her lips now. "I don't know what's happened, I don't know what you're talking about."

"You filled out your little assessment professionally, didn't you?" Alex spat. "Let the whole world know that you didn't think I was fit to parent Libby. Just when I was starting to think..."

She couldn't finish the sentence. Couldn't put into words what she'd started to think. Didn't want Kat to know now that she'd had feelings, that she'd wanted more, that she'd actually allowed herself to feel something for the woman.

"I didn't—"

"Enough, I don't want to hear it. No more lies. You can say that you didn't do it, but I'm not going to believe it. You've always judged me and now you're getting what you want, Libby taken away from me."

It hurt so much to say the words that Alex felt a cracking inside herself.

"And why? Because your sad little life is so boring, so lacking in anything, that you have to make trouble for someone else, is that it?" She was shouting now. "Because you can't have happiness, because your home got broken up, you have to break someone else's?"

"Alex..." Kat's eyes were filling with tears, her face had gone a green shade of pale and she looked like she was about to throw up. But Alex didn't care, couldn't care, not now.

"No. No Alex. No Kat. No Ms. Stein even," Alex said. "I'm done with this and I'm done with you. Get back in your car and drive away because I never want to see your face again." She took a threatening step closer. "And be warned, if I do see your interfering little witch of a face again I'll scratch your fucking eyes out."

Kat paused for only a second before she turned and fled, clambering into her car, starting the engine before the door was even closed properly.

Alex stayed on her feet, swaying, until Kat's car had screeched away.

And then she collapsed.

The cold dampness of the gravel under her seeped through her clothes. Deep, hiccuping sobs echoed in the night.

She wanted to feel betrayed, disappointed, hurt and broken and alone and all those things together. But there was so much there that she couldn't pick apart the pain. There was just a solid, throbbing mass inside her that felt like it was leaking from every pore.

Alex had no idea how long she lay in the parking lot. No idea how long she'd cried for. In the end, the only reason she got up, the only reason she got into her car, the only reason she stopped sobbing long enough to drive, was because Libby was at home waiting for her.

But who knew how much longer that would be true.

CHAPTER TWENTY EIGHT

She had been shaking so badly that she'd had to pull the car over and sob by the side of the road for what felt like hours.

Interfering. Assessment. Boring. Boring. Boring.

Oh, she knew that Alex was angry, she knew that the words were spoken in fury, not necessarily out of truth. But that didn't take the sting away from them. Didn't stop her remembering another night, not that long ago, when Jen had told her the same thing.

"Our marriage has settled," Jen had said. "We've fallen into a routine. I'm not denying that some of that is comforting. But I need more."

"Like Denise?" Kat had spat.

Jen had shrugged. "I'm not like you," she'd said. "I need more in life, more excitement. You're..." She'd tailed off.

"Go ahead, say it."

Looking down at the kitchen table Jen had finally snapped. "You're boring."

And now, in the cold calm of her quiet car, Kat heard all those words over again and more. But then, it shouldn't come as so much of a surprise, should it? She'd known she wasn't exciting enough for Alex. She'd suspected as much. She'd just kidded herself, let herself believe that maybe Alex was different, maybe *she* was different.

She should never have cracked her heart open wide enough for Alex to sneak in. That was the real problem. Her hands gripped the steering wheel hard, knuckles turning white, as she fought to gain control of herself.

Finally, she drove home, head aching with unshed tears. She should have known better. After Jen, she should definitely have known better.

When she climbed out of bed on Monday morning she was stiff with inaction. Fran had been gone all weekend, she'd had the place to herself, and she'd had plenty of time to think.

Logically, she knew that she'd had nothing to do with Olivia's bad assessment. Her own report had been stellar. On the other hand, she also knew how important Olivia was to Alex, and in that way could understand why Alex had lashed out, why she'd been so destructively angry.

Even now, she thought, as she drew her dilapidated car into the school parking lot, she'd forgive Alex if she walked through the door of her classroom. Even now, after an entire weekend crying and trying to put herself back together again, she wouldn't be able to help a smile if she saw her waiting at the school gate.

It was hope, she realized, as she got out of the car. Hope that kept her going. Hope that Alex would come and apologize, that her judgment would be proved sound, that she hadn't misjudged the woman, that she hadn't opened her heart to the wrong person.

She could put aside her personal hurt for long enough to see the strain Alex was under, the terror that her daughter would be taken away from her. Put it aside long enough for explanations and apologies. She would do that, she'd decided. She'd be the bigger person.

But the opportunity didn't present itself.

As the bell rang and children streamed into the classroom she painted on a smile and counted them in as though everything was perfectly normal. But there was one child missing. As she'd dreaded there would be.

"Good morning, class."

"Good morning, Ms. Stein," they chorused back.

"The first thing that we're going to do today is composition, so take out your best pencils and your composition books please."

She turned and wrote quickly on the whiteboard. This wasn't her lesson plan, she was doing this on the fly, but she couldn't help herself. Behind her, there was the shuffling and rustling of kids getting their books from their bags.

"Alright, class. I want you to write a short composition about what you did this weekend. There must be at least five sentences. And please remember the punctuation that we talked about last week. The beginning of a sentence must have...?"

"A capital letter," the class filled in.

"And the end of a sentence must have...?"

"A period."

"Very good."

She waited until little heads were bent over books before she opened the door that connected her classroom to the one next door. Trisha Benson's kids were already elbow-deep in paint.

"Keep an ear open for mine for five minutes?" she asked.

Trisha gave her a worried frown but nodded. She must look worse than she thought, Kat thought as she made her escape to the corridor.

The principal's office was quiet for a Monday morning. No one was waiting in the row of seats outside and the door was cracked open. Kat knocked.

"Yes?"

Ms. Martinelli had been principal of Brookfield for as long as Kat had worked there. She was formidable and strict, but with a twinkling kindness behind her glasses when necessary.

"Just checking in on a kid," Kat said. "Olivia Blakely? She didn't show up this morning and I know there's a custody battle going on so..."

"Quite right," the principal said. "I'd have been worried too. But nothing to be concerned about. I got a call from Ms. Blakely this morning."

"Oh," Kat said, heart jumping a little at the mention of Alex's name. "Olivia's not sick is she?"

"No, not at all. Ms. Blakely called to tell me that Olivia has been withdrawn from the school. I'll admit I was a little confused, but now that you mention a custody battle, it makes sense. Possibly she'll be moved somewhere that's more convenient for both parents."

"Possibly," Kat said, voice quiet and shaky. "Thanks."

She made it out of the office before tears escaped.

No hope.

She'd been foolish to have any.

No chance of Alex showing up and apologizing.

This was really all over.

The house echoed with emptiness when she finally got home. Fran obviously wasn't back from her weekend trip yet.

Kat kicked off her shoes and threw herself onto the couch. She was glad no one was home, she was glad for a little alone time. And maybe that was the point.

She was meant to be alone. At least for now. She was meant to be alone until she changed enough, until she became exciting enough, to deserve being with someone else. Or until she accepted the fact that she was boring and that she was better off without anyone.

The tears were gone. The hurt was there, burning and shining deep inside her. She blamed herself as much as Alex. If she hadn't been stupid enough to think that a woman like that, a woman as beautiful and exciting and spontaneous as that, would actually like her... If she'd just backed off as soon as she realized that there was no way she was going to be interesting enough for someone like that.

She sighed shakily.

No. Things had to change. She was coming to the end of the road here.

The fact was, she just couldn't have what she wanted. Whether that was Alex or her teaching job. And she had to face that fact.

She'd had that brief period of time when she was still married to a woman she loved and who loved her back, when she was doing a job she loved, when she was building a home, when she'd been happy.

But how much happiness did one person deserve?

Maybe she'd had her allotment already.

The options were closing in around her. And she could see only one path out.

Take the corporate trainer job. Quit teaching. Find her own apartment.

And stay single.

She took another deep, shaky breath. She was terrified, she was sad, she was alone. But she'd better get used to that.

CHAPTER TWENTY NINE

"Where are you going?"

Alex slung the suitcase into the back of the car and bent down to pick up the crate of toys Libby insisted had to come with them.

"Away."

Doug leaped over the small hedge separating their houses and jogged to the car. "Alex, this is not a good idea."

She ignored him and continued packing the car.

Doug had been there for her. When she got home he'd been waiting. When he'd seen her tears he'd comforted her. He'd heard the whole story and had been as sweet and loving as she'd needed. She appreciated that, she really did. But that didn't mean that he got to interfere with every element of her life.

"Alex, can I take some chicken nuggets?" Libby was standing at the door, a box of dinosaur nuggets in her hand.

"No, sweetie, not for a car trip."

"Please?"

The kid's lip was beginning to wobble and Alex had to bite her tongue not to yell at her, not to tell her she was being stupid and to put the nuggets back in the freezer. Then Doug stepped in.

"Hey, Lib, how about you go in and watch some TV. I'll help Alex with the rest of this stuff, don't worry."

"Really?"

"Really really, go on."

She clattered off and Alex glared at him. "My kid, my rules," she said. "I didn't say she could watch TV."

Doug reached up and grabbed the car trunk, slamming it closed. "Right now, Alex, you don't get to make the rules. I'm stepping in here."

"What the f—"

"No, come on, inside with me."

"No!"

"Alex, I'm about to stop you doing something you're going to regret for the rest of your life, trust me."

There was something in his voice that she hadn't heard before, a steeliness. She swallowed. "Fine. Five minutes. That's all I've got to give you. We need to get on the road before it gets much later."

He escorted her into the kitchen, closing the door on Libby and the TV, sitting Alex on a barstool and pouring coffee for the both of them.

"Alright, what's going on here?"

"I'm taking Libby on a road trip." Which was true enough in its own way.

"Alex, I'm a shrink. Do you think that people don't lie to me every day of the week?"

She sighed. "Fine. We're getting out of here."

"Running away?"

"Saving ourselves," Alex said. He made it sound like she hadn't put any thought at all into this. Of course she had. And it was a lot easier than she'd expected. Now that she had money, running away to a new place was a hell of a lot simpler.

"No," Doug said. "You're not saving anyone. You're making a huge mistake, one that affects not only you, but Libby as well."

"Doug—" she said, threateningly.

"No, Alex. I won't let you do this. You run away like this in the middle of a custody hearing and you're going to find yourself accused of kidnapping and child abduction. If you think your life's complicated right now, just you wait until you're the subject of a manhunt."

"Bullshit."

"No, no bullshit, Alex. I'm telling it like it is. This is one thing that you don't get to run away from."

"I'll go where the hell I like when the hell I like." She was starting to get truly angry now. Ever since Kat had betrayed her like that she'd been easier and easier to anger. It made her hot inside and tremble outside she was so furious.

"That's not how it works," Doug said. "And how would it look to the courts? To Libby's father? Did you think about that?"

"I don't give a fuck what they think."

"But you do, Alex. You do. You're a great parent, you want others to recognize that you're a great parent. I get that. But running away like this, taking Libby away from a stable home, a school she loves, making yourself a criminal in the process, what kind of parent does that make you? Hmm?"

Her fingers grasped around the mug before she knew what she was doing and Doug side-stepped just in time to avoid getting a face full of hot coffee. He caught her wrists.

"No," he said firmly, but calmly. "I won't let you do this, Alex. I won't let you run, I won't let you prove everyone else right about you. Look at yourself, look at who you were. A hippy who couldn't commit to a country to live in, let alone a career or a family. Of course people thought you'd be a terrible parent. But you've proven them wrong, you've built something here, you're doing amazingly. Are you about to throw it all away?"

His hand was tight around her wrist and Alex struggled to pull away but even as his fingers released her the anger was draining.

She wanted to run so badly. She wanted to go somewhere where none of this was happening. Where there was no Alistair Huston, no Kat Stein, just her and Libby and...

"Don't throw it away, Alex. You can't do this. Please, believe me, you can't do this."

She swallowed, breathed long, deep breaths. "Are you sure?"

she said. "Sure I can't go?"

"Very sure," Doug said. "You'll get into more trouble than it's worth. And... aren't you tired of running away? Haven't you learned anything yet about not running?"

"What do you mean?"

"Didn't you want to run when Libby was first awarded to you? Weren't you afraid then?"

She had a shuddering memory of a dark night in a motel right after she'd heard when she'd thought it might be better for everyone, Libby included, if she got on the next plane. She nodded.

"You were afraid, you wanted to run, and yet here you are now willing to do anything to keep the very thing that you were afraid of."

"I guess... I guess I don't always know what I want until I have it."

"You're no different than anyone else," Doug said. "And I don't doubt that you'll still have some form of custody of Libby, they're not going to take her from you. Unless you abduct her to fly her off to Cambodia or something, of course."

"Okay." Her voice was small.

"You have a lot of anger in you right now. A lot of it is directed at Kat, and she's not here to take it. That anger is only disguising your fear. You're not angry at the world, Alex. You're afraid of it."

"This has nothing to do with Kat Stein."

"Does it not?" Doug said. "Because if your judgment weren't so clouded perhaps you'd be a little more sympathetic to the position you put her in, and to the fact that no matter what, she did what she thought was best for someone that you love very much."

"Doug, I'm really not in the mood to talk about this."

"You need to get this stuff figured out. For Libby's sake and for your own. Whatever Kat wrote in that assessment, and I remind you that you have no idea what was in it, she wrote because she wants the best thing for Libby. Say she did write something bad, do you think that didn't pain her? To put aside her own wants and needs, the fact that she liked you, in order to tell the truth to protect a little girl?"

"Libby doesn't need protecting."

"That's not my point, Alex, and you know it's not."

"I can't do this, Doug. I can't forgive her. Not yet, not now. I... I need to focus on Libby. I need to sort my life out. Maybe you're right, I don't know. But even if you are, Kat Stein is the last thing on my mind right now."

"I get that." Doug grabbed another mug from the cupboard and poured more coffee into it. "And prioritizing is important. But don't let your feelings about one thing get in the way of your feelings about something else. You need to be strong and concentrate on the custody battle. That's it. Don't go making foolish decisions."

She took a breath and nodded. "I won't leave town."

"Good."

"But... I can't face Kat either. Not yet. I'm not sending Libby back to school."

Doug looked out into the backyard where frost was still lacing the grass. "I'm guessing it's close enough to Christmas break now that that probably won't matter too much. Though I'd probably re-register her in case anyone goes asking. She can start again in January, no? Give both of you a break."

Alex smiled a little. "Guess I got lucky moving in next to a psychologist, huh?"

"Maybe," said Doug. "Maybe you just got lucky moving in next to me." He winked and handed her the new mug of coffee. "Drink that. And then we'll go unload the car again."

Stay and face things. That was a new strategy. It scared the living hell out of her. But, she figured, she'd still have time to run with Libby if it looked like things weren't going her way. Running was a solid plan B.

CHAPTER THIRTY

Kat fingered the envelope in her hand. She was sweating, perspiration running down her back. Her pulse was thready, she felt sick, and her legs were shaking. But there was nothing else she could do. She raised her hand on knocked on the half-open door.

"Come in."

Ms. Martinelli had her glasses at the end of her nose, a pen in her hand, and a harried look on her face. But she smiled when she saw Kat anyway.

"Always nice to see you, Ms. Stein. Can I help you with something."

Kat took a deep breath, closed the door behind her, and sat down. She was still clutching the envelope and the principal raised an eyebrow at her.

"Is everything okay?"

"No. Yes. I, uh, here." With a tremoring hand, Kat slid the envelope across the desk.

"What's this?"

Her mouth was dry now but her eyes weren't, they were threatening to fill with tears. She could hear the shouts and laughter from the school yard and she couldn't believe she was about to say what she had to say.

"My resignation."

There was a long pause, a heavy silence that made Kat so uncomfortable that she didn't know where to look.

"I have to say that this comes as a surprise."

"I'm sorry." What else was there to say? She felt heavier, dirtier, just plain wrong, uncomfortable in her own body now that she'd done it.

"I'd always thought of you as a born teacher. Someone who belonged in a classroom. You'll be sorely missed."

Kat nodded.

"Is there anything that can be done about this?" Ms. Martinelli asked. "Any room for negotiation?"

"I, uh, I've taken a new job," Kat said. Her eyes filled with tears again and she blinked them away. "It's nothing to do with you, the school, the kids. I just... If I'm being honest, I can't survive like this anymore, not on my salary, not after the divorce."

Ms. Martinelli sighed. "I wish there was something I could do for you. But this is the way of things at the moment. Less and less money is being spent on education and we just don't have the budget to keep those teachers that really deserve to be paid more."

Kat stood up, wanting to get out now and so did the principal, walking around her desk. She laid a warm hand on Kat's arm.

"I'm so sorry," she whispered. "I can see how much this hurts you. I'm so, so sorry that we've all let you down."

"No," Kat said. "It's not you."

"It's the system," Ms. Martinelli said. "But still. The world needs teachers like you, Ms. Stein. And it's a loss to me personally, as well as to the school and a generation full of children that should have profited from a teacher of your caliber. You will be missed."

Kat's legs were still shaking as she walked out into the corridor, her eyes stung with tears, and laughter echoed from the playground.

"It's done?"

"Done," Kat said.

Fran pushed a glass of wine in front of her. The bar was busy but not too crowded. "You look like you need this."

Gratefully, Kat picked up the drink.

"To better times," Fran said, clinking her glass against Kat's.

"I wish," Kat said feverishly.

Fran shook her head. "It's been a rough year, Kat. Anyone can see that. But things are changing now. Maybe not in the way that you'd like, but that doesn't mean that your life has to be awful."

"Don't even try to talk to me about dating again," Kat said. "No way. No how. I'm done with women. I was very obviously meant to be alone."

"And don't you feel sorry for yourself?" Fran put her wine glass down. "I wasn't going to say anything about dating. In fact, quite the opposite, I was going to suggest that maybe you take a little time for yourself."

"O-kay..." The word came out stretched and long.

"Look, I get it, you don't want to give up teaching. But there are some benefits here, you know. You'll have more money. And you'll have more free time, no more bringing work home with you, when you leave the office, you'll be done. So why not take advantage of that?"

"What exactly did you have in mind?"

Fran scratched her nose. "Teaching is your passion, you love your kids. Without that, you're going to need to find something else to pour yourself into. And you're the one that's always complaining that you're boring. Not that I think you are. But you could use the extra time and cash to try out a few new things, maybe find something that you're equally passionate about as teaching."

"Alright, I guess I should be making the best of things."

Changing herself. Why not? It wasn't exactly like the old Kat had been such a success. Maybe Fran was right, she needed a little time to work on herself. Take a few sky-diving lessons or go scuba diving or something.

"I know you're upset, Kat. I feel your pain, I really do. But in the end, what can we do? We go on. That's the way of things. And if you're going to go on, then maybe it would be better to try and find a little happiness on your way."

She'd accepted it. Accepted that she wasn't going to have the wife, the home, the children. That wasn't what the world had in store for her. Did that mean she'd never be happy again? Of course not. Fran was right. She needed to find something for herself.

"Fine, I'll look into bungee jumping when we get home."

Fran laughed. "Not exactly what I had in mind, but whatever floats your boat." She held up her glass again.

Kat frowned but touched her glass against Fran's anyway.

"To a new start, a new you, and most of all, to finding the happiness that we deserve," Fran said.

Kat wondered just how much happiness she did deserve.

It was at night when things were worst. When there was no one else around and when she could let her guard drop and admit that she missed Alex.

Admit that as stupid as it was, as careless as it was, she'd given her heart to the woman. She wanted her. Even now, after the recriminations and the yelling and the insults, she couldn't help but see those blue eyes when she closed her eyes to sleep.

She wondered where Alex was now.

Olivia wasn't in school, so they'd probably gone away somewhere.

Maybe they were sunning themselves on a Tahiti beach. Or watching the sun rise over the Eiffel Tower. Maybe they were riding elephants or taking tea with Buddhist monks.

And as much as she missed Alex, as much as her body longed for her, Kat couldn't place herself in any of these fantasies. No matter what she saw Alex doing, she couldn't see herself doing the same. Which was the problem in the end, she supposed.

How could she ever have fit in to Alex's life?

Alex had done her a favor breaking things off like that. It would have ended badly, just as her marriage had. Alex had saved her an even bigger heartbreak.

Not that her heart wasn't broken, it was, but it could have been worse, she supposed. She could have been attached to Olivia, they could have gotten married, she could have lost her home again.

She turned into her pillow as the tears started again, hot and salty against her skin.

She'd decided she wasn't going back to school after Christmas. A handful more days and she'd be done. A little while longer and she wouldn't even have the comfort of shining happy faces smiling up at her every morning. Her heart broke again.

Fran said things could change for the better.

But it was very, very hard to believe.

CHAPTER THIRTY ONE

It was cold in the car. Three days after Christmas and she was sitting in a parking lot in front of a diner. She shivered.

"Just go in and listen," Doug said.

"Why?"

Doug sighed. He'd set this up, and she knew that he'd worked hard on it. "Because something tells me that the two of you want exactly the same thing," he said.

"Quite the little diplomat, aren't you?" Alex said.

"You've got nothing to lose."

"Fine," she huffed, if only to get him off her back.

The diner was at least warm, jazzy holiday music playing in the background, and she recognized him from behind, sitting in a booth, coffee in front of him.

"I'm here." It wasn't exactly graceful, but it was the best she could do.

"I see that," Alistair said.

His chin was so like Libby's, he even had a little dimple off to one side. Alex swallowed. This was for Libby, she reminded herself. "Sorry, probably should have started with hello."

He grinned now. "Maybe, but this is weird, I get that. Coffee?"

She nodded and he gestured to the waitress for another cup.

"I'm glad you're here," he said. "We, uh, we started off badly.

Things have kind of spiraled now, but I don't think it's too late to stop what's happening. I feel like you and I need to be brutally honest with each other and clear up a few misunderstandings."

"Misunderstandings?" Alex asked, accepting a cup of coffee. As far as she was concerned, she understood what Alistair wanted perfectly.

"I don't want to take Libby from you."

Or maybe she didn't. She put the coffee down just as she'd picked it up. "And yet you're suing me for custody."

He held up both his hands. "Okay, okay. I get that that sounds weird. But I don't want to take Libby from you. Can we..." He rubbed at his face with his hands, there was the rough sound of his stubble scratching his palms. "Can we take a second to start over? Let me explain maybe?"

Alex nodded, intrigued now.

"Alright, so, some of this you know. Claire told me she was pregnant right when I was leaving for Asia. She said she wanted nothing to do with me, that I had no responsibilities here. I'm not going to lie to you, a big part of me was relieved at the time."

He looked up at her and she understood completely the feeling he was talking about.

"That makes me sound like the asshole run-away-dad, but it's true. I didn't want to be tied down, I didn't want to have a child. I just wanted my freedom, my independence."

Finally, someone who got it. Still, she was wary. "Okay. But something changed."

He shrugged. "Not really. I mean yes, I changed. But walking away was a decision I regretted from the moment I made it. See, I wanted to be independent, but I knew that I had someone, a child, who was mine and I missed everything. Walking, talking, everything. I would have gone back, I think, had Claire not been so definite that she didn't want me involved."

"But what about being free and easy, being independent?"

Alistair laughed. "Not all it's cracked up to be. It's lonely being alone, you know that? And apart from anything else, these things we think tie us down, they anchor us, that's all.

Give you something to love, something to believe in. I saw plenty of families in Hong Kong, plenty of other bankers took their kids and their wives. I'd seen things as black and white, free or not free, but there's always a compromise, isn't there? For the right person."

Alex's heart beat harder. She'd been willing to compromise for Kat, she knew she had. She'd already had thoughts of traveling with her. Since the fight she'd been consoling herself with the idea that at least she wasn't going to be tied down, but... But what if Alistair was right? What if she needed someone like Kat to anchor her.

"Let's face it, it's nicer to have someone to come home to at the end of the day, isn't it? It took me a while to realize that a child, a family wouldn't have tied me down. The only thing tying me down was my own attitude and misplaced beliefs." Alistair was saying. He rubbed his face again. "So, I regretted what I'd done. Enough that when I got back here the first thing I did was look up Claire. I was hoping... I don't know, for something, another chance. Then I found out about the accident and my daughter and you and... And I got scared."

"Scared?"

Alistair nodded. "I think so. I didn't know you, you wouldn't answer any of my phone calls. When I finally did come to visit you, you threw a cup of tea at me."

"Coffee."

"I didn't get the chance to taste it," he said with a grin. "So maybe I over-reacted a little. I've read all the assessments, all the reports, I know that you're doing an amazing job, that you're the perfect mother for Libby."

Nobody had ever said that to her before, and she was shocked at how... beautiful it sounded. Perfect. Tears came to her eyes.

"I don't want to take her from you, Alex. But I do want to be part of her life. We need family, in the end it's all we have, whether it's the family we're born into or the one we build ourselves."

She had a flash of an image, her and Kat and Libby playing

in the garden. Something they'd never done. Because she and Kat had always been careful to keep their relationship entirely away from Libby, not wanting to confuse her. They hadn't tried to build a family, they'd kept secrets and deliberately kept the family divided. And she couldn't help but think of Kat.

There's been a lot of time over the holidays to consider everything. To think about what Doug had told her, that whether her assessment had been good or bad, Kat had put everything aside to do what was best for Libby. He'd been right. But Alex still hadn't been able to call, hadn't been able to apologize or anything else. It was over, she'd said terrible things, and she couldn't face what she'd done.

Yet Kat was in her mind more often than not. The memory of her skin, her taste, her eyes. The thought of what could have been. When the anger was gone, burned away over time, she was left with a vision of Kat that was haunting and taunted her late at night. She loved her, she already knew that, had accepted it as though it was a universal truth. She loved her but they couldn't be together. They were just too different.

But now she had to know. "Those assessments you read, one of them wasn't good."

Alistair frowned then nodded. "Yeah, there was one. All of them were close to perfect but there was one from the school that said Libby wasn't always dressed appropriately, that she'd been in fights. It was from uh..."

"Ms. Stein," Alex said, her heart falling through her stomach.

"No," Alistair said, looking surprised. "A Ms. Martinelli, or something like that. The school principal." He saw the look on her face. "But it was all about nothing, she was just covering her ass, everything checked out just fine."

It was like all the oxygen had been sucked out of the diner. The tinny music still played but it was all she heard as the world circled around her.

Kat hadn't done it.

Kat didn't think she was a bad parent.

Kat approved of her.

It shouldn't matter, but it did. Suddenly it mattered more than anything else in the world. Suddenly she knew that she needed to find her, needed to apologize, needed to take her in her arms and tell her that she wanted to be anchored. She could do tied down, for green eyes and a truthful heart that could never lie or cheat.

"Alex, you okay?"

She nodded.

"I think we should try and work this out between the two of us. I think Libby should have both of us in her life. Could we try something like that? Please?"

She stared at him. Compromise. Balance. It all slid into place now. She could have everything. She could have Libby, and she could have free time and independence as well. Doug had told her long ago that all children needed balance, but maybe adults did too. Maybe Kat did as much as she did. Maybe that was why the feelings were so strong even though they were both so different, maybe they needed each other to complete the picture.

Alistair was looking down at the table, and when he looked up she saw a glint of tears.

"Alex, please. I want to be a part of my daughter's life. I know I screwed up and made bad decisions in the past, but I'm here now and I want to make amends. I swear to you that I'll never hurt her, that I'll only do what's best for her. But please, please give me another chance to make this right."

Slowly, Alex nodded. "Yes," she said. "A compromise. A balance. I think Libby would like that. I'd like it."

Alistair grinned at her but she didn't see him.

All she saw was Kat.

She'd said unspeakable things in her anger. Kat might not want to see her. But she could try. She wanted to try.

Because suddenly the idea of building a family didn't sound bad. A different kind of family, maybe. A family that traveled over the vacations, and if her new business idea panned out there was going to be plenty of traveling. A family that was on time and polite and disciplined, but that also knew how to swim in the rain and laugh and leave their responsibilities behind when the time was right. A family that was tall and blonde, and short and dark. A family of opposites that blended together purely because they were so different, because they needed each others' differences.

She gave a hiccuping sob. She'd fucked up with Kat so badly. How could she ever make things right again?

"This is none of my business," Alistair said. "But are you alright?"

She shook her head and the story of Kat came pouring out of her. And when she was done he was smiling at her.

"What?"

"Go get her."

"What if she doesn't want me?"

"Alex, we all make mistakes, just like I did leaving my daughter behind. The only thing we can do is realize our mistakes and ask for forgiveness and a second chance, just like I'm asking you. And if my stubborn ass can ask for a second chance, yours certainly can."

She hesitated.

"Life's all about risk, Alex. There are no sure things."

She nodded. Then she nodded again. Then she got up and ran back out to the car.

CHAPTER THIRTY TWO

Her chair had wheels and could spin, both of which were a step up from her old classroom chair which had one leg shorter than the others. The office seemed cold and lonely though. After a lifetime in classrooms decorated in primary colors and finger-paintings, bare white walls were cold.

"Not bad, no?" Jackson said. He was leaning in the door frame and grinning at her.

"It's lovely," Kat said, swallowing down her disappointment and sadness. She really was trying to make the best of this. "And I owe you my thanks, getting the hire date pushed up like this was really helpful."

Jackson shrugged. "You're the right candidate, we wanted you. Besides, you won't start here proper until February fifteenth, we've got a couple of training courses we want to send you on first. But we're truly glad to have you on board."

"Thank you," she said with a grateful smile.

He scratched his head and looked less smooth than usual. "I, uh, I was wondering if perhaps you'd like to, um, grab a drink or something after this?"

Kat stared at him with her mouth open. This was not what she'd been expecting. She'd made it a practice over the last few weeks to say yes to everything, but this... even she couldn't say yes to this. Opening up her life to new things was all very well, but...

"I, um, I can't, I'm sorry."

"Maybe next week some time?" he pressed.

Kat took a breath. This had never really been a problem before. She'd never had to come out at work before. Seven year olds didn't ask you for drinks after work. Best to start the way she meant to go on though, she guessed.

"I'm gay." It just blurted out. Not that that was the only reason. She was staying solidly single. Single for at least eighteen months, she'd promised herself.

Jackson grinned. "Immune to my charms then," he said goodnaturedly. "No problem. I'd still be happy to have that drink as friends though, if you'd be comfortable with that? We could ask Fran along too?"

"Sure thing," Kat said. "Next week would be great."

"I'll leave you to it here then," he said. "Just don't forget to lock the door when you're ready to leave."

The office was so quiet. The building was so quiet. She had known that things were going to be different, but this... She sighed. She should go home. Home to her new empty apartment. Not exactly something she was looking forward to. Her phone rang.

"Hey, it's Jen."

Kat let out a breath. Not that she hated Jen, she'd long ago forgiven her. But Jen only really called when she needed something. "What can I do for you?"

"I've got a bunch of plants here that I think you might want. House plants, that is. You want them, or..."

Kat thought about her empty apartment. "Yes, definitely."

"We're just clearing out for the move," Jen said. Kat's heart cracked a little, but she'd known that Jen and Denise were getting a place of their own, that the little house she'd loved was going on the market. "How about you pick them up tomorrow night?"

"I've got salsa class tomorrow," Kat said. "And book club the night after."

"Aren't you the social butterfly?" Jen said.

"Well, you're the one that called me boring," said Kat, the words slipping out before she could stop them.

There was a long pause. Then Jen said: "Listen, why don't you meet me at that coffee shop we used to love? I'll bring the plants. Say in a half hour or so?"

Her voice was a little softer, a little sadder, and Kat agreed because she was too busy wondering why Jen's tone had changed.

"It's good to see you," Jen said, standing back a little to get a good look. Kat felt examined. "Grab a table, I'll get some coffees."

No need to tell Jen her order, she always had the same thing. Kat wanted to be sad or mad or something, but she couldn't be. Jen looked good. Happy, fit, confident. Happier than Kat had seen her look for a long time. It was more than that though. She knew now that Jen hadn't been right for her.

Alex, that was who she really wanted. The woman that didn't want her back.

She jumped as Jen put coffee cups on the table.

"Listen, this is odd, I get that, but I've been meaning to talk to you for a while," Jen said.

"You have?" asked Kat.

"I need to apologize to you. For... for how things ended."

Kat shook her head. "We don't need to do this, Jen."

"Yeah, yeah we do. It's important. What you said on the phone, about me calling you boring. That was a shitty thing to say, not least because it's not true, it was never true. I guess... It's easier to see things at a distance."

"Perhaps." Kat was now just confused.

"Our marriage ended because I wasn't happy," Jen said. "I can't speak for you, but our relationship wasn't giving me what I needed. And blaming you for that was taking the easy way out. I think I forgot somewhere along the line that it takes two to make a relationship."

"Apparently three in our case," Kat said sharply.

Jen flushed but plowed on. "Kat, we just weren't meant to be. Some things aren't. We made a mistake, both of us together. It happens. I don't regret what we had. For a while there I was really happy, and I'd like to think that you were too. But then I wasn't. I can't explain it. Maybe I changed in the wrong direction, maybe we both changed, but it just wasn't working anymore. I do know one thing though."

"Which is?"

"You're not boring, Kat. That was a shitty excuse and something I never should've said. You have so much going for you. I didn't fall in love with you for nothing. You're smart, attractive, and you're good at the difficult things in life. Better than I ever was at things like making a home. I'm sorry for what I did, for what I said, but I'm not sorry that we're divorced. It was the right thing to do. Staying together would only have made things worse."

Kat took a deep breath then nodded. "You're right. I didn't think so at the time, the pain was concealing everything else, but splitting up was the right choice. Calling me boring though, I don't know. Maybe you were right. You do all these exciting things, like kite surfing, I just like to stay home and read. I am boring."

"Nah," Jen said. "Going out and doing stuff, that's not being interesting. Being interesting is being able to talk for hours about nothing at all, it's being able to have new ideas and opinions. The kite surfing and whatever else, that's just icing on the cake. It's fun, sure, but those things aren't what make a relationship. I don't love Denise because she goes surfing with me. I love her for the same reason that I once loved you."

"And what's that?"

"Damned if I know," Jen said with a grin. "Hormones? Biology? Not a clue. What makes one person love another? It's just an attraction that won't go away, a sense that this is what's meant to be. I like her because she makes me laugh, she makes me feel safe, she makes me a better person. I love her because... because that's just the way it is. Like the sky is blue. I can't explain it."

Kat smiled a little and Jen reached out to take her hand.

"I'm sorry for the hurt. I'm not sorry for the good times though. And Kat, you're many things, but you're absolutely not boring. Anyone that can stay up all night talking about nothing and make it so riveting that sleep seems impossible can't be boring. Or maybe that only happens when you're in love."

Her apartment was silent. She really needed to get some more furniture, but the plants helped. She made herself some tea before bed.

So Jen didn't think she was boring after all. Well, that was something, she supposed. Alex still did, which was the more important thing now.

She was trying to fill her life, to better herself, to take salsa classes and cooking classes and all the rest, just as Fran had suggested. And she felt better about herself for getting out there. But that didn't stop the hole inside her that she needed to fill. The hole that she'd thought Alex was the perfect fit for.

It had taken her a long time to get over Jen. In fact, she hadn't really gotten over Jen until she'd met Alex. It seemed like it was going to take longer to get over Alex. And not for the first time, she wished she could have a second chance.

Her hand hesitated over her phone as it had done a million times before. But she just couldn't do it. She couldn't call Alex. She couldn't face Alex's wrath, couldn't face being turned down again, or even worse, Alex not picking up at all.

With a sigh, she plugged her phone in to charge and took her tea up to bed.

CHAPTER THIRTY THREE

The envelope lay on the kitchen counter and Alex couldn't face opening it. In the end, Doug was the one that slit it open and Alex held her breath as he read the letter.

"You got it."

"I got it?"

"The loan is yours, they completely approved your business plan, you got yourself a company!"

Doug grinned and pulled her into a hug. The idea had been bobbing around for a while now. Organizing tours of lesser known destinations for the more adventurous traveler. It had taken a while, and some solid help, to get a real business plan put together and now the loan was in and she felt like she'd really accomplished something. So why didn't she feel better about herself?

"What's going on?" Doug asked, pulling back.

"I—I don't know."

"I feel like you should really be happier about this. You and Alistair are on your way to solving the custody problem. You're starting a new business. It finally looks like you've got all your ducks in a row."

"Except for one thing."

Doug smiled a little. "Kat."

Alex nodded.

She'd done her best to put all of this out of her mind. She'd gotten afraid, had lost her certainty for a moment. So she'd tried to just forget about Kat, thinking maybe she was a phase, maybe things were better this way. But it wasn't working, it just wasn't.

"So, what are you going to do?" Doug asked.

Alex looked at him, looked at the letter in his hand, cocked her head to see Libby's dark curls as she sat watching TV. She almost had it all. But none of it was making her happy. Because there was no balance. Because something was missing.

"Get her back."

"Those are big words," Doug said. "Sure you can live up to them?"

"No," said Alex. "But I'm sure I have to try. I fucked up. I fucked up because I was scared and angry and because I didn't know where I fit into the world. And I took it out on Kat. So at the very least I need to apologize to her. And then, maybe, hopefully, she might give me a second chance."

"And if she doesn't?"

"Then I'll have to live with that," Alex said stoutly, not at all sure that she could.

"Got a plan?"

"Nope."

"Well, sounds like you know exactly what you're doing," Doug said.

"That's kind of the point. I don't. But that's okay, it's okay to go in without a plan sometimes, it's okay to feel things out, to be spontaneous."

"That and you're so afraid of jinxing things that you don't want to think of what might happen."

"That too," Alex said with a sigh. "But it's the first day of school on Monday, so I'd rather find out sooner than later."

Doug held her hand and squeezed it. "You've done a lot of growing up and it suits you. But remember, we still don't always get what we want."

"I know that. But I also know that in general, we get what we need," Alex shot back. "And I'm going to do my damn best to show Kat that I need her and that she needs me. I can't stop thinking about her, Doug. She's like some kind of drug. I crave her. And when I think of what I did, how I screamed at her, I want to sink into the earth. I don't know how she can ever forgive me."

"It's more important that you forgive yourself."

"I won't be able to do that until I at least apologize."

"Fair enough," said Doug. "But you do know that if you're planning on talking to Ms. Stein on Monday morning there's a pretty big hurdle to overcome first."

"What's that?"

"Well, you're going to have to tell Libby that she can't catch the school-bus."

Alex pulled a face. "I think I'd rather face a pack of rabid dogs."

"She's a good kid. She'll understand," Doug said. "She's calming down a lot now. Having a stable home is good for her. Meeting her father was good for her. She handled it well, which is a credit to you and the stability you've given her."

"Maybe."

Doug laughed. "You're a good mom, Alex, you don't need to be shy about admitting it sometimes."

Libby was dancing as Alex held her hand and walked her across the parking lot. Alex felt like her stomach was dancing. She hadn't been so nervous since... Since the first day she'd had to take Libby home.

"Excited about your first day back, huh?"

"Sooo excited," Libby said, drawing the word out. "I love it here. Thank you, Alex."

"For what?"

"For letting me go here."

The playground gate was open and Libby slipped her hand out of Alex's and ran off to join her friends. Alex stared after her.

She hadn't really realized until that moment how important it was for Libby to be here, to have a school she loved, to have friends and a routine and things to count on. But she guessed she could understand why. Having her whole life ripped away from her when her mother died meant that she placed more value on things that stayed the same.

The thought that she'd nearly not let Libby come back made her feel a little sick.

The school doors were open and Alex walked slowly inside, still trying to decide what she was going to say to Kat. She was afraid. Afraid that Kat was going to turn her down, afraid she was going to screw this up. She was afraid that at the first sight of the teacher all the feelings were going to come flooding back stronger than ever, afraid that they wouldn't come back.

By the time she reached the classroom door, she was shaking and could barely open the door.

"Can I help you?"

Alex stood in the doorway, glancing around the classroom as though she'd made a mistake. But no, this was the right place, the view, the furniture, it all looked the same. The only thing that was different was the young man standing by the whiteboard.

"I'm looking for Ms. Stein," she said.

He smiled. "I'm afraid Ms. Stein doesn't work here anymore. She left at the end of last year. My name's Rob, I encourage the kids to call me by my first name, I'm the new second grade teacher."

It was running away. Alex recognized it because that's what she'd always done. Running away from your life to try and get something new when in reality all that was necessary was a small change or two.

Not that she could blame Kat for running. She'd done it often enough herself. Until right now. Until she finally realized that no matter where she ran to, or how often, or what she ran from, she was still going to be herself. It was still her doing the running and nothing would change because she wasn't changing.

She tapped her fingers on the steering wheel, trying to think. She needed to get hold of Kat, but how? She'd already tried the principal's office and got nowhere. Ms. Martinelli, who frankly Alex still blamed for sending in a negative assessment, refused to give out personal information.

She had Kat's number, of course, and even her email address, but she was afraid that Kat wouldn't answer, wouldn't give her the chance. She had one shot at doing this properly and she was desperate to get things right.

She was resolute now. Finding that Kat had quit the school had made her see how very, very wrong they'd both been, about each other and about themselves. Kat belonged at Brookfield Elementary, and Alex was determined that she would return.

Kat belonged with her. Not that she knew it yet. But she would, Alex would make her see the truth, make her see that she, Alex, deserved Kat.

But how to do that in a way that didn't seem impersonal or traditional or stalker-y or anything else? She wanted to do this in person, but that wasn't going to happen.

She tapped her fingers on the steering wheel again, thinking. There was one thing that might work. Maybe. It was worth a shot anyway.

There was one way in which she and Kat had always communicated well, where there'd never been any yelling or arguing, where they'd seemed to slide perfectly together like pieces of the same jigsaw.

She picked up her phone. It was the best shot she could think of.

The app took forever to open and her message box was empty. Not that she'd expected differently. She opened up a new message field and typed in Kat's screen name. Then she took a deep breath and started to type.

CHAPTER THIRTY FOUR

Sweat was trickling down her spine and beading on her forehead. Kat gulped greedily at her water bottle, legs shaking with tiredness and every muscle aching.

"Remember, keep those shoulders still," the salsa instructor was saying. "Hips move, shoulders don't."

Kat grinned and the woman next to her dug an elbow into her ribs. "I wouldn't mind moving his hips," she hissed.

"Eleanor!" said Kat, pretending to be shocked.

The older woman grinned back. "There's life in the old dog yet."

"As for Saturday," the instructor went on. "You've got all the info you need in the email I sent you. If you don't have the email then come see me right now. Long story short, we'll be meeting at the Eastside Mall in the far back parking lot at two for a quick warm up. That's it. Thank you, class."

"You ready for Saturday?" Eleanor asked as Kat bent to get her sweater.

Kat shrugged. "Ready as I'll ever be," she said, though in truth she was nervous as all hell. She'd joined the salsa class slightly late and had always felt like she was chasing to catch the others up.

"You'll do just fine, it's gonna be fun."

"It'd better be," Kat said, stomach doing flips at the thought of it. But that was the price of living an exciting life, you had to do things that made your stomach turn somersaults.

"Feel like a drink tonight?"

Despite her vow to yes wherever possible, Kat shook her head. "Not tonight. I had a late one last night with some people from my training course. I need a bath and bed."

"Next week then."

"For sure."

Kat picked up her bag and slung it over her shoulder, shouted a goodbye to several other women in the class that she'd come to know, and made her way out of the dance studio to her car.

She was happy with herself for this, for making the commitment, for taking the time out of her schedule to learn to dance. Happy enough that she was seriously considering heading down to Mexico when she could finally take a vacation. Alone. That was the biggie. Her first vacation with no one to rely on but herself.

Not that it should be that hard. She was a grown adult and free to do as she pleased. But how the hell was she supposed to fill all the hours in a day without anyone else there? The question lurked in her mind and she had no idea how to answer it.

"Ah crap," she said as she deposited her gym bag in the car and caught sight of the bookstore sign. She'd meant to go pick up the next book for her bookclub but had arrived late enough to class that she hadn't had time.

She hesitated for a moment. That bath sounded terribly tempting. But in the end, it was better to do it now. She was already here, she needed to get started on the book, and why waste the gas on an extra trip?

The bookstore was brightly lit, fluorescent lights making Kat blink as she stepped in out of the dark, cold evening. But it was warm and busy, comforting in the lull of chatter as customers looked over books. There was even the sharp scent of coffee coming from somewhere.

It took all of two minutes to find the book that she needed, but Kat spent an easy extra twenty looking at other shelves, and eventually turned around with a pile of five books in her hand. Only to bump straight into a little figure.

"Oh, I'm sorry, sweetie, are you okay?"

The child's face was pale, her eyes darting, and Kat instinctively knew that the girl was close to panic. She could only be around five, her blonde hair fine and blue eyes starting to tear up. Kat squatted down, gently touching the girl's arm.

"I know you shouldn't speak to strangers," she said softly. "But I'm a teacher. I teach second grade. I think you might be lost. Are you lost?"

The little girl nodded miserably.

"Alright, you don't need to worry. I'm going to help you. You take my hand and we'll go find your mom or dad. We won't leave the store, I promise you that."

The kid hesitated before she took Kat's hand and Kat unconsciously decided she must have good parents if they'd taught her to be so aware of strangers. Small fingers curled into her own and slowly, Kat walked toward the children's section.

They were only half way there when the child ripped her hand away and started running toward a harried looking woman in the middle of the kids' section and Kat relaxed a little as she saw the woman bend to hug the child, then stand up again to scold her. All safe.

But the memory of that little hand in hers hurt. All around her kids were playing, looking at books. There was the sweet descant trill of young voices and more than anything Kat wanted to clap her hands and have the children gather round her, wanted to tell them stories, straighten their shirts, hand out tissues for runny noses.

It was an urge so strong it was impossible to do anything but just stand there, watching. She missed teaching so badly, missed her kids so much, it was like a physical blow to the stomach. Her eyes stung with tears and she could barely hold them back.

"Ma'am, are you alright?"

A concerned looking member of staff approached her and Kat sniffed. What a sight she must look. Hell, how scary and sketchy she must look. A middle aged woman crying in the children's section of a bookstore. She sniffed again.

"Perfectly fine," she said sharply. She held up her pile of books. "Just looking for the cash desk."

"Right this way, ma'am," said the clerk, leading her away from the children.

But she could still hear them. And she knew now that she'd made a terrible, terrible mistake leaving teaching. A mistake that she'd had to make, that she'd had no choice but to make, but a mistake nevertheless.

There was nothing she could do now. All the salsa classes and trips to Mexico in the world wouldn't make up for the fact that she'd had to leave her one true calling.

The notification sound was both familiar and strange. She knew the noise, but it took her a moment to place it, to remember what it signified. And when she did, she rolled her eyes.

Reaching a soap-sud covered arm out of the bath tub she dried her fingers on a towel and picked up her phone. She really needed to delete the dating app. Not that she'd had much luck with it, but still, if she was going to remain single it was better to have a clean slate.

She opened up the app to get rid of the message notification, her heart skipping a little at the thought of LexyLibre.

Every time she tried to put Alex behind her, something happened to bring her back to mind. It was impossible. She was just going to have to live with the ghost of Alex haunting her every day, she guessed.

Except.

She blinked.

Except...

She blinked again, sure she was imagining things.

But she wasn't. The message center wasn't exactly complicated, she could see immediately who had sent the message. Her heart stopped and her mouth dried up. Her finger shaking she pressed the icon to open the message.

> LexyLibre>> *Some things need to be said in person. Some things should never be said at all. But some things demand to be told. Forgiveness is too much to ask, but perhaps closure isn't? Meet me. Please. I can't close my eyes without seeing you.*

She had almost been willing to write the message off, right up until that last line. It was only with that last line that she knew Alex was in as much pain as she was.

That didn't mean they should meet though.

She'd sworn off women, sworn off relationships. She was recovering. Slowly, too slowly, but seeing Alex now could set her back weeks, months. Alex wouldn't want her back. What was the point?

"No," she said out loud, voice echoing in the bathroom. "That's the old Kat."

The old Kat was boring, the old Kat stuck to the rules. The new Kat, the slowly evolving person she wanted to become, had more confidence than that. Okay, Alex might not want her back. But closure was necessary. Just as it had been with Jen, just as she and Jen had needed to talk things over in that coffee shop, she and Alex needed the same.

Not that Kat had any intention of meeting Alex in a coffee shop. An idea was beginning to form. Maybe she needed to give Alex a glimpse of what she was missing. Let Alex see that she was changing. Risky, scary, but she needed this, needed someone to recognize that she was pushing herself now, that she wasn't the person she used to be.

Her fingers were still shaky as she typed.

> KittyKat>> *Be at the Eastside Mall, Saturday, 14.30, second floor overlooking the food court.*

Her heart was thudding in her chest as she set her phone

down.

What had she done?

With a groan, she closed her eyes and slid gently back down into the bath water.

CHAPTER THIRTY FIVE

Alex paced the balcony, back and forth, back and forth, until the staff member at The Gap started giving her funny looks.

What was she doing here?

Maybe it was a trick, some kind of prank? Her heart had skipped when Kat had finally sent a message and she'd allowed herself to hope for just a moment that maybe there was something here to be fixed. But a meeting at the mall?

She sighed. Maybe Kat felt better meeting her in public, not that she could blame her for that. Smells wafted up from the food court below and she leaned on the railing. Where was Kat? She scanned the crowd below but didn't see her.

Suddenly, there was a loud vocal trill. Loud enough that the mall stood still for a second, that the chattering of busy shoppers stopped. Alex's heart was pounding. Then a beat started, oddly familiar, catchy and staccato. She frowned.

Below, the crowd was moving, but seemingly in a pattern now and she couldn't quite put together what was happening. A buzz of chattering rose again as people looked and pointed and suddenly, there they were.

A host of dancers, streaming out as the music got louder and louder. Then, as one, the group moved, and like a snake shimmering along the ground began to dance. And Alex laughed.

A flash mob.

She'd always wanted to be in one but had never had the chance, or the balls to be honest. She wasn't the best dancer. She looked around quickly. Kat would be mad that she missed this. But her eyes were drawn back to the dancers, to the sinuous shapes they were making, to the strong beat of the Latin music, to one spot in particular.

One spot where a tall, blonde dancer was moving along with the rest.

A dancer that Alex only now recognized.

Her mouth fell open.

Could it be?

No.

She had to get a closer look.

She pushed her way through the crowd watching from the balcony, grappled her way to the escalator and jogged down it, thrusting and shouldering through yet more people until finally she came to a spot where she could almost see.

It couldn't be.

She pushed closer and closer.

Just in time.

Just as the dancer's arm clipped a stray chair and her foot slipped and then her leg went from under her and Alex's hand shot out and she absorbed the impact of someone falling and then... Then she was holding Kat in her arms, the familiar shock of electricity crackling between them, the sense of a circuit being completed.

She breathed in once, enough to fill her sense with Kat's smell. Then she let go, pushed Kat back out there.

"Finish this!" she hissed as Kat stumbled back into place and picked up the steps as the show came to a crescendo.

Kat. Kat of all people doing this. Alex watched the way her body moved, swelled with pride as the teacher swooped and curved with the other dancers, thrilled inside as the spectators clapped and cheered.

There was no bow, no encore, the music came to a crashing end and the dancers simply walked away, blending back into the crowd as Alex felt green eyes turn to her, bore into her soul.

"You caught me."

Alex nodded.

"Thank you."

And Alex wanted to say that she'd always catch her, that she wanted to be the net that Kat relied on, but she couldn't, didn't.

"I looked for you at school."

"I quit."

"I heard. It seems... wrong."

Kat shrugged. "We don't always get what we want. Finances were tough, I needed a better paying job, that simple."

That didn't sound at all like Kat. But Alex brushed it aside, took a deep breath. "Please, will you sit with me for a minute, there are some things that I need to say."

Kat hesitated, then nodded, sitting down at a small food court table.

"I don't know where to start."

And there was Kat's smile, just a small one, but enough to give Alex the courage she needed. "Start at the beginning," Kat said.

"I should never have said the things I did. I know you didn't write a bad assessment for Libby. But even if you had, you would have done so only to protect her. Because it would have been the right thing to do. That aside, I spoke out of anger and I don't deserve to be forgiven for what I said."

Kat shook her head. "Words are words, Alex. Not actions. Don't feel so sorry for yourself. We've all said regrettable things in the past. I'm glad you're apologizing though. Thank you. Apology accepted."

Alex let out a breath. It was strange being here, sitting so close to Kat, having her be real instead of in her imagination. And then her mouth just started moving, words started spinning out of it as though she'd lost all control, as though she was drowning in Kat's eyes.

"I love you," she said. "I love you, Kat and I think I always have. I've made so many mistakes and I've been so horrible and I don't even know if you could ever love me back, but I have to tell you."

She could see Kat's hands trembling, but she said nothing, so Alex went on.

"I think I'm supposed to come here willing to sacrifice anything to have you back, but I can't, because that's not the point. This whole time, I always thought that settling down, having a girlfriend, a home, kids, was all about sacrifice, giving things up. But it's not, is it? It's about gaining, adding to what you already have. I want to give us another try, because together we can be so much more than we are separately."

Kat took her hand. "I don't know, Alex. I don't know if—"

"I understand," Alex said. "This new you, the you that does flash mobs and dancing and isn't a teacher, she's different. I understand if you changing means you don't want me anymore."

"It's not that. I changed because... Because I needed to," Kat said. "Because I realized that I was boring, I was boring myself. I needed to get out, to live life before it passed me by."

Alex was struck by a thought. "You didn't change for me, did you?" she asked. "I never, never want you to change for me."

"No," Kat said, with a laugh. "I changed for myself, not for anyone else."

"We're so different," Alex said. "But we balance each other out. Sure, there are plenty of things we don't agree on, but is that such a bad thing? I think I can help you become more... free. I think you can help me become more, um, grown up maybe. I—" She stopped herself.

"You what?" Kat said, leaning in temptingly so that Alex wanted to kiss her.

"I've started a business," she said. "Sorted out the custody stuff. I'm making in-roads. I'll still travel, but less, I'm starting to like the feeling of responsibility."

"I've started doing flash mobs," Kat said. "Apparently, anyway. And to be honest, I kind of like being the center of attention every now and again."

"I was always so afraid of settling down, becoming boring. But this isn't boring at all, it's exciting. I thought you were judging me as a parent, but to be honest, sometimes I could use that judgment, sometimes I could use someone calling me out for doing things wrong, because I don't always know what I'm doing."

"Sometimes I could use someone calling me out for being boring," Kat said with a shrug. "Someone to challenge me to do something new, to take a risk, to live life in the now sometimes."

"There's something missing in my life," Alex said. "And it's you. I know it's you. I understand if you want nothing to do with me. But I'd like a second chance. Please."

Kat sighed and looked away. "A second chance."

"I'd like to start over. From the beginning. I want to do things properly this time. I want you, Kat, and I'm willing to do whatever it takes to get you back as long as you want me." She took a breath. Here goes nothing, she thought. "But if you don't want me, just say, and I'll walk away for good, I swear."

Still, Kat said nothing. Alex's whole body shook.

"A new beginning. Right from the start," Kat said finally. "Building something together."

"If you want to," Alex said. "But doing plenty of things apart as well. Having some balance there."

"Maybe I could do that," Kat said. "I, well, I'm enjoying working on myself, to be honest. I'm liking myself more."

"There's only one condition," said Alex.

"Which is?"

"Whatever the cost, however we have to work this, you need to go back to teaching. I don't believe that you're happy outside of a classroom. We'll find a way to make it work."

Kat didn't say anything, her eyes were sparkling with tears

and she was leaning in again and this time the intention was unmistakable. Alex bent towards her, their lips close to brushing.

"You found her!" said a shrill voice. "You found Ms. Stein!"

Alex looked up to see Libby running toward them, Alistair in tow.

"Sorry," Alistair said. "We're a little early, we were just going to get some ice cream while we waited, but she saw you and..."

"And it's fine," Alex said, watching as Kat hugged Libby to her.

"Where did you find her?" Libby demanded of Alex. "Is she coming back to school?"

Alex shot a glance at Kat. "That's up to Ms. Stein," she said. "Entirely her decision. But there is something that you should know. Ms. Stein and I are friends, a special kind of friend. I thought that maybe we should invite her to dinner tonight."

Libby nodded eagerly, and Alex grinned.

"So, what about it, Ms. Stein? You in the mood for some family dinner. I'm pretty sure there's enough dinosaur chicken nuggets for three."

A hand reached across the table, fingers entangled with hers. A warmth flowed through Alex's arm and down into her stomach and Kat's smile made her shake inside. And then she knew that it was all going to be okay. That everything was going to be just fine.

"Dinosaur nuggets are my favorite," Kat said, looking down at Libby. "But only with broccoli."

"Yuck," Libby said, sticking out her tongue.

"Have you tried it?" asked Kat.

"Yes, it's yucky."

"Well, let's give it another try tonight. You should always give things a second chance." Kat looked up at Alex. "It's quite easy to make a mistake the first time."

Alex grinned back. There was a strange feeling in her chest. It took a second before she recognized it. It was the feeling of her heart being full to overflowing.

EPILOGUE

Kat twisted her hair up and stuck in a few more pins. There were never enough pins as far as seven year olds were concerned. She gave her head an experimental shake and her hair felt secure enough. Stepping back, she surveyed herself in the full length bedroom mirror, turning sideways on and examining her profile.

She was sure. She just didn't know how to bring the idea up with Alex. From the bedroom across the hall she could hear the regular arguments about what Libby could pack and what she couldn't. She grinned. Libby was going to win this battle, she always did when Alex was concerned.

"I'm getting a cup of coffee and then I'm ready to go," she shouted through. "Anyone that's not ready gets left here."

She heard Libby groan as she went down the stairs. It was the last day of school, for Libby the last day of third grade. And not for the first time, Kat was incredibly grateful that she'd gone back to teaching.

It had been a process. She's spent six months with Fran's company before agreeing to move into Alex's house. And only then when Libby herself had invited her. Then she'd gone back to teaching, just as Libby started third grade that September. And things were working out, more or less. Except for the parts that weren't working, obviously.

She sighed. This was important to her, desperately important, she just didn't know how Alex was going to take the news and... And they'd been doing so well for the last year and a half she didn't want to rock the boat.

But rocking the boat was the only way she was going to get what she wanted.

Hands steady, she grabbed the travel mug from the dishwasher and filled it to the brim with piping hot coffee. Securing the lid, she picked up her pile of marking and then went to stand by the door.

"Let's get out of here," she yelled.

Libby came half-tumbling down the stairs, followed by Alex who was still in her pajamas.

Kat opened the front door and Libby spilled out. Alex came closer and as her lips neared, Kat turned so that they brushed her cheek. Her heart broke a little as she did, but she couldn't not. She couldn't look Alex in the eye. Not right now. Not while she was still holding this truth in her chest and couldn't find the words for it.

"We'll meet you at the airport later," she said as she walked out the door.

※ ※ ※

Alex watched the car drive away.

Something was wrong. She knew it. Kat knew it. Even Libby was starting to get antsy about things. But she was damned if she knew what exactly wasn't right.

Kat had been quiet, snappish and short when she did speak, for a couple of weeks now. Maybe more. Alex rubbed her face with her hands.

Business was going well. Her first set of tours had gone out in February to places she'd traveled to herself. And other than a few teething problems, all was well. She planned things, made arrangements, and called on people she knew to guide the tours as they passed through certain places. She had the contacts, she had the experience, and she was thoroughly enjoying herself.

Not that it hadn't been hard work. She'd been working on a new Asian project for the last three months and it had meant many sleepless nights.

Maybe that was Kat's problem. Maybe she'd been neglecting her.

Just when... Alex rubbed her face again.

There was a knock at the door.

"Hey there, neighbor."

Doug was sweaty in his running gear and bore her mail, which Alex took. "I've got a Skype meeting in fifteen," she said. "No time for coffee."

"I've got a patient in a half hour," Doug grinned. "But I do need that spare key otherwise your plants definitely won't get watered."

Alex smacked herself in the forehead, she'd completely forgotten.

"You look like you've lost a dollar and found a nickel," Doug said as she searched through the bowl by the door for the spare key.

"Too much work, not enough time. Too much stress."

"Well, you've got a whole summer to get over that."

"Mmm. Maybe." She found the key and handed it over. "We appreciate the help, seriously. Thanks for keeping an eye on the place."

"No worries. When you guys get back I'm slavering for an invite to the wedding. Just remember, I need to be seated next to unattached attractive male cousins. Or uncles. Hell, I'm not picky."

Alex tried to smile, but she couldn't summon one up in time. Doug's eyebrows raised.

"You didn't ask her yet," he said.

Alex shrugged. "The time wasn't right." And likely never would be at this rate. Not with how strangely Kat was behaving.

"Take your time, Alex. There's no hurry. This is a big step for you, for both of you. Just... be patient."

She managed a sickly grin this time before she said goodbye and closed the door on him.

She wasn't sure there was ever going to be a right time

* * *

"Libby, can you run these to the principal's office, please," Kat said, handing over her attendance book and some paperwork.

"Sure thing," Libby grinned.

"And come straight back here," Trisha Benson said, a warning tone in her voice.

Libby skipped off and Trisha shook her head.

"I swear, that child would wander to the moon and back if left to her own devices."

"She takes after Alex," Kat said, with a laugh. "I have to tie her to the cart every time we go to the supermarket."

Trisha laughed. "It's nice to see you happy," she said.

Kat had a shiver of guilt. Was she happy? Truly happy? That was the question she'd been wrestling with for so long.

The answer was no. She wasn't.

And she didn't know how to make herself happy without compromising what she had with Alex. Alex and her dislike of responsibility. She couldn't add to Alex's weight, couldn't give her more to be responsible for.

"So, what are the big plans for the summer?" Trisha was asking.

Kat blew out a breath. "Well, Libby's going to be spending six weeks with her dad, which is a first for her, but she's terrifically excited about it."

"So I've heard," Trisha said. "In fact, she won't stop talking about it. Are you ladies going to be okay with an empty house?"

Kat's stomach shivered. An empty house. It didn't have to be empty.

"Uh, yes," she said. "We won't be there for a lot of the time. We're off to Mongolia and Tibet, some tour that Alex is trying to put together that we need to try out first."

"Sounds a hell of a lot more exciting than Disneyland," Trisha said.

And more dangerous and riskier, thought Kat. She swallowed down the fear inside her. Pushing herself to do new things, letting Alex push her to do new things, was important. She could master her fear, she knew that now.

If only she could master it enough to spit out what was on her mind.

But the thought of losing Alex was more terrifying than anything else in the world, scarier than prop planes and robbers and bungee jumping and anything else combined.

There was the sound of little feet trotting down the hallway. Kat picked up her purse. "I've got to get out of here, or Libby's going to miss her flight."

"See you in September," Trisha grinned. "As long as you don't fall off your yak or decide to stay in a monastery somewhere."

Kat laughed. A monastery actually sounded pretty good right now. At least she'd get some peace and quiet, something she could use after a whole year of rowdy second graders.

* * *

Alex crouched down and clutched Libby to her. "I'm going to miss you, kiddo."

"It's okay, Alex, you've got Kat, you'll be okay. And I'll be okay with daddy. Do they have dino nuggets in Singapore?"

Alex laughed. "I've got no idea, sweetie. But I'm sure they've got lots of cool stuff. Especially ice cream. It's gonna be hot there. Make sure you wear your sunscreen."

"I will. There's Kat. Kat!"

Kat came running to the gate. "Here you go, Olivia," she said, handing Libby a bottle of water.

Libby never complained about it, Alex thought. She didn't seem to mind Kat calling her Olivia, though it had taken six months before Libby had felt able to call Kat 'Kat' and not 'Ms. Stein.' They had a special kind of relationship, and Alex had noticed that whilst she was Libby's go to person for hugs and cuddles, it was Kat that Libby turned to for advice.

But now even Kat was hugging Libby. "You be a good girl."

"I'm always a good girl," Libby said. "And you have to look after Alex, 'cos she's sad."

There was a moment of silence when something really should have been said, but it wasn't. Kat said nothing and Alex's heart cracked a little. She swallowed back her sadness. "I'm not sad, I'm glad you're getting to spend time with your dad. It's important. And, if I'm not mistaken, your escort is coming right now."

There were more hugs and a few minutes of chaos as they handed Libby over to the flight attendant that was going to take care of her on the flight and then, suddenly, it was all over, and it was just the two of them walking through the airport.

Alex desperately wanted to reach out for Kat's hand, but she couldn't. She was too afraid that Kat would pull away. Afraid that this was all going to be over now. So afraid that she didn't know what to do with herself and tears were stinging her eyes.

She stopped in the middle of the concourse.

"What?" Kat stopped too.

Alex took a deep breath. She was terrible at this, horrible at communicating the important things. But she was working on it, with Doug's help, and this, right now, this was important. She needed to know, needed to tear the band-aid off.

"We need to talk. Now."

Kat frowned, but Alex paid no attention. She took her arm instead and steered her toward a seat.

Another deep breath. "I don't know what's going on. I just know that something's wrong. Something with us. Is it about me working too much? Is it about our trip? We don't have to go, you know. If you don't want to go to Mongolia, if it's too much for you, then just say so. If you want me to work less or quit altogether, just say so."

"No, no," Kat said quickly.

A third breath. Alex could barely form the words now.

"Then it's me," she said. "You want to leave me." She looked up and her view of Kat was clouded by tears. "I can't stop you. I know that. But I can beg you. Please don't go, Kat. Please. I'll do whatever you want."

Again there was that hesitation and then Kat was pulling her close and Alex didn't know what the hell was happening but she didn't care, she just cared that Kat's arms were around her and that she could smell her scent and feel her heart beat.

It was a long minute before Kat let her go.

"I've screwed this up," Kat said. "I was afraid, too afraid to tell you. And now you've got all the wrong idea and I... I don't know how to fix this."

"Tell me," Alex said. "Whatever it is, just tell me and we can fix it together."

"There's nothing to fix," Kat said. "I... I love you Alex and I love Olivia and our life, but there's something missing."

Alex's stomach lurched again. "Okay," she said numbly. "What is it?"

Kat looked her deep in the eyes. "A baby."

A lex took a deep drink of the wine and Kat smiled at her. It was something that she liked about Alex, her ability to recover quickly, her ability to stand up and face something.

"Why didn't you tell me?"

The airport bar buzzed around them and Kat felt her face flush. "Because... Because I didn't know what you'd say. I know you didn't really want kids in the first place, and that responsibility is hard for you. So I thought if I told you I wanted a baby then you'd just see it as me making you settle down even more."

"Jesus, am I that bad?" Alex said.

"No, no, I just... I've been stupid," Kat said.

"Kat, you have to understand, I've changed. You've changed.

That's the greatest thing about us, together we're better than we were separately. And no, I won't agree to you having a baby."

A freezing shiver of cold air passed over Kat. Had she been wrong? Should she have kept silent? But Alex was reaching for her hand.

"But I will agree to us having a baby. The two of us. Together. This isn't something you do on your own."

"What about settling down?"

"Psh, you think I can't ride a yak with a papoose on my back?" Alex said. "Our baby's going to be the best traveled kid in the world."

Our baby. The words made Kat feel warm and gooey inside. "You're the second person that's mentioned yaks to me today. Everyone seems convinced that I'm going to ride one."

"You might," Alex said. She was gripping tight on Kat's hand now. "But since we're on the subject of things we've been afraid to say, there's something that I've been terrified to say for a while now."

Kat raised an eyebrow. "Is this about the car thing? Because I don't see the point in buying a new car just for the sake of having one. I'm perfectly happy with my old banger, thank you very much."

"No, it's not about your car," Alex laughed. "It's about us. I, uh..." She took a deep breath. "I was, um, wondering if you'd maybe think about marrying me?"

She shouldn't have doubted herself. She'd known in one exact moment how perfect this was. She'd slipped while she was dancing in the flash mob, Alex had come out of nowhere to catch her. But it wasn't the catching that sealed the deal. It was the fact that once she'd been caught, Alex pushed her straight back out on the floor and told her to finish her dance.

That combination of safety and challenge was what she loved about Alex, loved about the way Alex made her feel. And now, under the fluorescent lights of the airport, the smell of liquor sharp in her nose, weary travelers surrounding her, she couldn't think of something that was more perfect.

A long, long time ago she'd lost a perfect life. What she hadn't realized was that in order to be perfect a relationship had to have its imperfections as well, there had to be a comparison, downs to go with the ups.

"You know, you're everything I never wanted," she said.

Alex grinned. "Right back at you. So, what do you say? Shall we get hitched and make a baby?"

"You make it sound so romantic."

"Doves and rose petals seemed out of place in an airport bar."

Kat laughed. "Yes," she said. "Absolutely, one hundred percent."

"Thank God," Alex said. "Now we only have to convince Libby that having two Mrs. Steins will be better than one."

"Oh, I don't think that'll take much persuading," said Kat. "Although how she'll take being a big sister, I'm not so sure."

Alex looked down at her watch and then screwed up her nose. "You know, as much as I like hanging out in airport bars, and as romantic as this little proposal was, we have packing to do and a nice house with a big bed at home. What do you say we take this party back to our place?"

Our place. Our baby. Our family.

Kat stood, picked up her purse, then held out her hand for Alex.

And hand in hand they walked out of the airport and into the coolness of the evening.

THANKS FOR READING!

If you liked this book, why not leave a review? Reviews are so important to independent authors, they help new readers discover us, and give us valuable feedback. Every review is very much appreciated.

And if you want to stay up to date with the latest Sienna Waters news and new releases, then follow me on **Twitter @WatersSienna** or on **Facebook**!

Keep reading for a sneak peek of my next book!

BOOKS FROM SIENNA WATERS

The Oakview Series:
    Coffee For Two
    Saving the World
    Rescue My Heart
    Dance With Me
    Learn to Love
    Away from Home
    Picture Me Perfect

The Monday's Child Series:
    Fair of Face
    Full of Grace
    Full of Woe

The Hawkin Island Series:
    More than Me

Standalone Books:
    The Opposite of You
    French Press
    The Wrong Date
    Everything We Never Wanted
    Fair Trade
    One For The Road
    The Real Story
    A Big Straight Wedding

Or turn the page to get a sneak preview of Fair Trade, the latest release from Sienna Waters...

FAIR TRADE

Chapter One

The squeal of brakes came a millisecond before the force that propelled Leigh forward so hard she smacked her head on the seat in front of her. She just about heard the screech of metal as she was flung back into her seat again.

Heart beating hard, head throbbing, a knot of fear in her stomach, she didn't even have the wits to scream.

"Jesus, you wanker, look where you're going can't you?"

Without even checking to see if she was alright, the driver climbed out of the cab and started yelling and gesticulating in the middle of the street and Leigh closed her eyes and tried to block it out. This wouldn't have happened, she thought, if she'd bothered to wait for a real London cab, a black cab, rather than stopping the first mini-cab she saw in the street.

She'd just been so anxious to get away.

Her head throbbed again and she felt a pain in her shoulder where the seatbelt had yanked her back. Could this day get any damn worse?

It hadn't started off particularly badly.

The air was crisp and cold, the morning dulled with a smoky fog. Exactly the kind of English morning that she loved. The kind of morning that made her thank her lucky stars that she'd settled here rather than anywhere else in the big world.

Winter was coming, and with it would come cozy sweater weather and reading in front of the fire weather and long nights of warm comfort. Nights when no one would expect her to do anything, when there'd be no neighbors grilling in the yards, no guilt pushing her to go from a run by the riverside.

She sighed with contentment as she locked the front door behind her and started her commute.

A decade she'd been in London and she still felt a quiet excited thrill at the smells and sounds and sights of it, so different from Oregon. Thankfully, beautifully, totally different from Oregon.

She reveled in the fact that no one looked her in the eye as she waited for the tube. No one smiled as she joined the other commuters in the train carriage. No one batted an eye as she walked up the huge escalator at her station.

Not that the English were cold exactly, they just... had a way of pretending that things didn't exist unless they were forced to directly confront them. A fantastic characteristic, in Leigh's opinion. No one interfering or telling her to smile or touching her arm to make a point.

"Morning, Ms. Hudson."

Leigh nodded at the receptionist as she pushed through the glass and metal doors of Llewellyn & Banks. The same brassy-blonde haired woman had greeted her every day for the last two years and she was damned if she knew the woman's name but she didn't care.

Isolated, some would say, happy in her own company was how Leigh preferred to think of things. Safely wrapped up in her own little world with no need for anyone else to try pulling at the strings or scrabbling at the tape with their grubby fingernails. Independent. Strong.

"Eight?"

The man who strode into the elevator after her smelled of Old Spice and neither smiled nor met her eye.

"Yes."

Her response was brisk, cool, and factual only. Despite the

fact that the two of them must have taken a hundred or more elevator trips together.

Not a single word more was spoken as the elevator glided upwards. Then the doors slid open and Leigh made her way to her office.

"Queen Bee's on the war-path," Jemima said as Leigh stopped long enough to hang up her coat.

That was the first hint that something was wrong. Not that her boss was on the war-path, that was never news, but that her assistant had greeted her with anything other than the formal 'good morning, Ms. Hudson' that she normally got.

Leigh grunted in reply, displeased at the break in protocol, and went to her desk where the morning's work already awaited her, planned, as usual, the evening before. She pressed the intercom on her phone.

"Coffee," she barked to Jemima.

Then she opened her computer and began sifting through her mail as it booted up.

She recognized the official logo of the UK Visa and Immigration office in the top corner of an envelope. With a steady hand, she propped the envelope up against the edge of her monitor. She was well aware of the fact that it was only a reminder to extend her visa, the actual expiry date as well as the optimal date to apply for a renewal were already marked in her diary.

Still though, another hint that today wasn't going to be the stellar day she had initially thought.

The third hint came storming through her door about three seconds later.

The Queen Bee, as she was known around the office, was Leigh's direct superior. She took pride in her nickname, knowing what everyone called her, thinking it meant that she was the head of the pack. But Leigh knew, as did everyone else in the place, that Queen Bee was just a way of making Queen Bitch sound slightly more polite. The Bee was less of a buzzing insect bee and more of a letter B. B as in bitch.

"I'm surprised you'd show your sorry face in here this morning," was the first thing she said.

"I'm sorry?"

"After the complete hash you made of the Harrison case. I spent a shitty breakfast meeting this morning with the main client and frankly, I'd be surprised if you'd done any research at all on the damn negotiation. You left me looking like I was sitting there with my right tit out in the cold."

Leigh swallowed. The Queen Bee's dirty mouth was legendary and she'd never warmed to the idea of a woman speaking to her that way, a man either for that matter. She thought about the hours of work she'd put into working on the Harrison analysis, the late nights, the early mornings. Her fingers had cramped up at the keyboard one day she'd been typing so much.

"Nothing to say for yourself, eh?" The boss folded her arms. Her dark hair was brushed back in a french twist, her eyes were hazel and ringed with make-up. Once, long ago, Leigh had even thought her attractive. Now she was just a bitch.

"I'm, uh, sorry."

She knew what Bee wanted, so she gave her as much humility as she could even though she knew she hadn't screwed up the analysis. More likely Bee hadn't even read the carefully put together file in the first place.

"You're skating on thin ice, little Miss," Bee said, her teeth clenched. "Don't push me. Another fuck up like this and I'll have you out on your arse."

She turned and left and Leigh knew this wouldn't be the end of it. Bee would hold this over her head for weeks, even though she was sure the file had been correct. She was also sure that as a corporate lawyer her skills were being vastly under-utilized for simply running background checks and going over paperwork and researching backgrounds for negotiations.

"Here you go," Jemima said, coming in with a coffee. "I waited until she was gone."

Leigh took the coffee but said nothing. Jemima hesitated, her skirt just a little too short, biting her lip. Then she spoke again.

"I'm sorry. I know you worked hard on that file. You shouldn't let her speak to you that way, you know."

"Mind your own business," snapped Leigh.

She saw tears welling in Jemima's eyes and looked away. Really. She felt a spike of guilt at making the girl cry but it was important that she learned her place in the world.

As Jemima stumbled out, Leigh's eye caught the envelope sitting on her desk. Visa. She knew damn well that Bee wanted to fire her, knew that Bee had taken against her for a million reasons. Not least because she never socialized or went on office retreats or drank and bitched with the girls.

What she hadn't connected until just this second was that if she was fired, her work visa would become invalid.

An invalid work visa would mean eventually being deported.

And that would mean running back home to mommy and daddy with her tail between her legs.

Her heart started to thud and she felt a band tightening around her chest. Her breath came faster and her lungs wouldn't fill properly and a dizzying blackness was beginning to creep into the corners of her vision.

Back to Oregon. Back to the commune. Back to...

She could barely breathe now. The walls were moving in on her, the ceiling pushing downwards. With a shaking hand, she grabbed her briefcase. She had to get out of here. Now.

"Dentist," she managed to gasp to Jemima as she fumbled for her coat getting one arm in and then abandoning the idea and simply wrapping the other half of the garment around her. Outside, fresh air, cold, that was all she could think.

"But—" Jemima started, nose slightly stuffed from stopping her tears.

"Dentist," Leigh said again with all the force she could muster.

And then she was walking away, banging through the emergency door to the stairs and fleeing the scene.

Fresh air had helped. And then she'd decided that she was owed a day off after all the extra hours she'd put into the Harrison case, and then she'd decided that she wasn't going to walk all the way home in her heels, and then she'd hailed a mini-cab.

And then the cab had crashed.

Her head still throbbed, the driver was still arguing, and Leigh unbuckled her seatbelt. A few yards down the road she could see the familiar swinging sign of a pub.

She didn't bother to glance at her watch, she knew it couldn't be much later than ten thirty. And she didn't care. Suddenly she couldn't face going back to an empty house.

She needed a drink.

Chapter Two

There was something about the city in the early hours of the morning that Rosie loved. She was no sadist. Getting up at three wasn't something she longed to do. The cold of the bare wooden floorboards soaked through her socks and slippers and she shivered her way to the gas stove, coffee was the only way to get warm.

But the empty streets, the soft grey of dawn, the cheerful smiles of the street cleaners and dustbin men and other early workers were all special. This was a London that no one else knew. This was a happier, friendlier city, one that was safer and softer and more pleasant to be in.

The van cracked as she moved it down a gear.

"Come on, Big Bess," she cajoled, wiggling the gear shift just a bit.

The van responded with a touch more speed and she grinned. Bess was older than she was, but there was life in the old girl yet. She turned into a narrow street and turned again into an alley, bringing the van as close as she could get to the flower market.

Life as a market gardener wasn't exactly luxurious. She jumped out of the van, jeans caked with dirt at the knees, boots stained, her well-loved jumper unraveling at the cuffs. Up at three, out in the allotment by half past, flowers cut and arranged by four, and off to the market before the sun was even up most days.

That didn't mean she wasn't happy though.

Sometimes, like right now, she inhaled the scent of a million flowers and her eyes stung at the colors and she felt like the luckiest damn girl in the world.

"Over here, Rosie!"

A hulk of a man was waving at her and she jogged over to him carrying her first two crates. "Morning, Joe."

Joe, affectionately known around the market as 'The Gentle Giant', slapped her on the back and flashed her a grin. "What's new, pussycat?"

"Since this time yesterday?" she said, putting the crates down. "Not a sausage. You?"

"Well, you know, late night. Angelina didn't want to cut the date short and insisted we go to The Ivy for supper and then had to have a ride in the old Ferrari, and after, well... A gentleman doesn't kiss and tell."

"Angelina?" Rosie said, setting the crates out. "Oh, Jolie."

"That's her," said Joe. "I don't know how I'm going to break it to young Kiera that I've fallen for an older woman."

"Kiera Knightley, I'm assuming?"

"That's the one," Joe said, shaking his head sadly.

"You're a prat," Rosie said. "But a lovely one." She stood on tiptoes and kissed his cheek. She wouldn't be where she was without Joe. He'd shown her the ropes, protected her stuff, helped her get started. And she loved him like a brother. Quite a bit more than her brother, actually, given that her brother was an arrogant prick. "Let me get the rest of my stuff."

The morning was cold, definitely the coldest of the year so far. Rosie shivered and pulled her old jacket around her torso. Summer was definitely gone then. She sighed as she went back to Big Bess for another load.

The colder months weren't her favorite. Her business growing and selling English wildflowers was precarious enough in the summer months. In the winter it was practically non-existent. She'd better start looking for some café work to pick up the slack.

She was wondering where to apply as she went back into the big market hall.

"Must have been freezing your bits off in that shed this morning," Joe said as she came back to her pitch.

"It's not a shed, it's a cabin."

Joe snorted. "It's a shed, love. You're not on the electric, you're not on the gas, and I don't even want to know where you take care of your bodily needs. A bucket under the bed, I'm thinking. You know that once the council catches on to what you're doing you'll be out on your ear."

"In which case, I'll go back to sleeping in the back of Big Bess," Rosie said, stoutly. "And the council haven't caught me for the last year and a bit, so they're not going to be catching me now, are they?"

Joe sighed. "Fine. Bring your washing 'round tomorrow if you want."

Rosie grinned in thanks. Yes, there were inconveniences to living off grid, but she did her best. A swim and a shower at the local pool once a day, laundry at the laundrette or at Joe's if he was feeling generous, and a chemical camping toilet. No problem was without a solution.

"Uh-oh, here comes trouble," Joe said.

The market hall was starting to fill up, buyers from florists, hotels, wedding planners and even some normal passers-by were coming in and starting negotiations. Rosie had a small niche, but a few regular clients, some of the hipper boutique hotels that liked to buy English and stuck to more environmentally friendly wildflower options.

She looked through the throngs and frowned, not understanding, until she saw a red head bobbing toward them. Her stomach sank. Cassandra Reed.

"Morning Joe, morning Rosie," Cassandra said with a sweet smile. "Things are looking lovely over here as usual. It can be easier to work with such a small selection, can't it?"

Rosie gritted her teeth and grunted. Small selection. Given the allotment that she was working with she did the best she could. Mind you, if she had thousands of pounds donated by an over-generous father then maybe she'd have her own damn garden center just like Cassandra did.

"Not got enough to do?" Joe asked.

"The girls know how to take care of things," Cassandra said with another sweet smile.

"Must be tough having someone else to do everything for you," sniffed Joe. "Hard to get good help these days, isn't it?"

Cassandra ignored him, turning her eye instead to Rosie's pitch. "Those are some nice red campions you've got there, Rosie. You should think about putting them in your Clover's display."

Anger boiled tight and hot in Rosie's stomach and she closed her eyes for a second, not even able to bear looking at Cassandra. Clover's Flower Awards were highly sought after, very prestigious, and could make or break a gardening career. They were also, as Cassandra well knew, limited to only professionals, meaning only gardeners who had a corporate identity could enter.

Cassandra with her garden center would be chomping at the bit to get her flowers in for the competition. Rosie could only dream.

"Don't be a bitch, Cassandra, there's a love," Joe said.

"Oh, right," said Cassandra, her smile turning saccharine-sweet. "I forgot. You're not eligible, are you? Oh well, maybe next year."

She waltzed off and Rosie waited until she was out of ear-shot before blowing a loud, rude raspberry at her back.

"Ignore her, Rose, you know she's only trying to wind you up."

"I know, I know."

"And she's right about one thing, there's always next year. Who knows, maybe this time next year you'll be in all the magazines and have your own center. Can't predict the future, can you?"

Rosie snorted. "I can. Right now I can't even pay rent on a flat, let alone afford to rent premises and start my own garden center. There's not a chance in hell of that changing in the next twelve months. Not without a miracle."

"Heavenly miracles exist," said Joe. "Don't knock 'em. You never know when it's going to be your turn to get blessed by the good luck fairy."

"Blessed?" Rosie said, shifting a few more crates. "I think she mugged me in a dark alley and stole everything I have. Bloody fairies."

Joe laughed.

The market got done early, most punters gone by nine. It took a while to clean up, and Rosie needed to move Big Bess or else get a parking ticket. After that, it was lunch with Joe and then back to the allotment to get to work.

Not that there was much work to be done at this time of year, but she could always find something in the small garden to keep her entertained.

She circled around an accident at one side of the street, an irate taxi driver yelling at another car while broken glass and dented metal sparkled in the morning sunshine. Then she lucked out with a nice parking spot just a few feet later.

It was about half past ten when she walked into the pub on Bridge Road, their usual lunch spot. Early, but the pub was used to early customers coming in from the market. And if you got up at three in the morning, half ten was around about lunch time. Rosie's stomach was growling anyway.

Joe wasn't in yet, and looking around neither was anyone else, so Rosie sat herself down at a table to wait. She noticed the woman at the next table only because she looked so out of place. A smart suit, high heels, short blonde hair sleeked back and expensively cut. What was someone like that doing in a place that had a sticky floor and smelled of last night's beer, she wondered.

There was a snuffling sound.

It was a few seconds before she realized that the blonde woman was crying.

Order Your Copy of Fair Trade Now!

Printed in Great Britain
by Amazon